How easy it would ... *to grab her free hand, to haul her back to him, wrap his arms around her, kiss her again and again and again.*

But he didn't.

Somehow, he kept his head.

She turned when she reached the doorway to the sitting room. "See you tomorrow." She quietly shut the door behind her.

He sank to the edge of the bed, wondering what he had gotten himself into.

Thinking he should call the whole thing off.

And knowing he would do no such thing.

Dear Reader,

Travis Bravo's mom is determined to find him the perfect woman. And she doesn't listen when he asks her, repeatedly, to stop matchmaking, *please.* He's loved and lost and he's not going there again. Now he just wants to go home for Thanksgiving without having every pretty debutante in San Antonio waiting to meet him.

He comes up with a plan. Yeah, okay, his strategy involves a great big lie. But still. It's a harmless lie, one that hurts no one. All he needs is the right woman.

His good buddy Samantha "Sam" Jaworski is the perfect choice. He talks her into helping him out a little. Sam's a soft touch. She'll do anything for a friend, and Travis is about the best friend she's got. Plus, Sam wants to make a few changes in her life.

They come to an agreement. She'll go home with him for Thanksgiving and help him get his mom off his back. He'll help *her* spiff up her image and find a new job.

It sounds like a great idea. Until they begin to discover more about themselves—and their true relationship— than either of them bargained for.

Happy holidays, everyone!

Yours always,

Christine Rimmer

A BRAVO HOMECOMING

CHRISTINE RIMMER

Harlequin®

SPECIAL EDITION

ISBN-13: 978-0-373-65632-5

A BRAVO HOMECOMING

www.Harlequin.com

Printed in U.S.A.

CHRISTINE RIMMER

came to her profession the long way around. Before settling down to write about the magic of romance, she'd been everything from an actress to a salesclerk to a waitress. Now that she's finally found work that suits her perfectly, she insists she never had a problem keeping a job—she was merely gaining "life experience" for her future as a novelist. Christine is grateful not only for the joy she finds in writing, but for what waits when the day's work is through: a man she loves, who loves her right back, and the privilege of watching their children grow and change day to day. She lives with her family in Oregon. Visit Christine at www.christinerimmer.com.

For good men and true-hearted women everywhere.
May your holidays be filled with good cheer,
family togetherness and much love!

Chapter One

"Honey, are you seeing anyone special?" Travis Bravo's mother asked.

Travis stifled a groan. He should have put off calling her back.

But he'd already done that. Twice. In a row. Aleta Bravo was a patient and understanding mom, and she got that he wasn't real big on keeping in touch. But she did have limits. After the third unreturned call, she would have started to worry. He loved his mom and he didn't want her worrying.

Besides, when Aleta Bravo started to worry, she might get his dad involved. And if his dad got involved, steps would be taken. The two of them might end up boarding a helicopter and tracking him down in the middle of the Gulf.

No joke. It could happen. His parents had money and

they had connections and when they tracked you down, you got found.

So now and then, he had no choice but to call his mom back, both to keep her from worrying *and* to keep from getting rescued whether he needed it or not.

She was still talking, all cheerful and loving—and way too determined. "I only ask because I have several terrific women I want you to meet this time. Do you, by any chance, happen to remember my dear friend Billie Toutsell?"

He did, vaguely. Not that it mattered if he knew the woman or not. He knew what she had.

Daughters.

At least one, probably two or three.

His mom continued, "Billie and I go way back. And I've met both of her girls. Brilliant, well brought up, beautiful women. Cybil and LouJo. It so happens both girls will be in town for Thanksgiving week…" *In town* meant in San Antonio, where his mom and dad and brothers and sisters still lived. "And I've been thinking it would be nice to invite both of them out to the ranch over the holiday weekend, maybe Friday or Saturday. What do you think?" Before he could tell her— again—that he didn't want to be set up with any of her friends' daughters, she went right on. "Maybe Billie and her girls would even like to come for Thanksgiving dinner and our reaffirmation of vows."

After forty years of marriage, his parents were reaffirming their wedding vows, which was great. They'd had some troubles in the past few years, even separated for a while. He supposed it made sense that they would want to celebrate making it through a tough time, coming out on the other side still married and happy to be together.

But did his mother have to invite him *and* every available single woman in south Texas to the big event?

What made him so damn special? His mother had six other sons and two daughters and they'd all been allowed to find their own wives and husbands. In fact, as of now, he was the only one who had yet to settle down. That, somehow, seemed to have triggered a burning need in her to help him find the woman for him.

Hadn't she done enough? She'd already introduced him to both of his former fiancées. Rachel, whom he'd loved with all his heart, had been killed eight years ago, run down by a drunk driver while crossing the street. He'd thought he would never get over losing her.

But then, three years later, he'd met Wanda at a family party, over the Christmas holidays. His mother and Wanda's mother were friends. He shouldn't have gotten involved with Wanda. But he had. And it had not ended well.

Evidently his mom thought the third time would be the charm. "Oh, Travis. I'm so glad you'll be there."

"Wouldn't miss it," he muttered. "But, Mom, listen. I really don't need any help finding a girlfriend."

"Well, of course you don't, but opportunity is everything. And you're always off on some oil rig somewhere. How many women are you going to meet on an oil rig?"

"Mom, I—"

She didn't even let him finish his sentence. "It's been years. You have to move on. You know that." She spoke gently.

"I *have* moved on."

She sighed. And then she said briskly, "Well, it never hurts to meet new people. And, you know, I've recently been acting as a docent—twice a month at the Alamo. It just so happens that I met a lovely young woman there, also a docent, Ashley McFadden. I know you and Ashley would hit it off so well. She's perfect. Great personality. So smart. So funny."

Travis winced and sent a desperate glance around the lounge. He could a use a little help about now. He needed someone to rescue him from his own mom.

But rescue was not forthcoming. He was alone with a wide, dark flat-screen TV, a row of snack and drink machines, random sofas and chairs and a matched pair of ping-pong tables. Across the room, a couple of roughnecks were Wii bowling on the other TV. Neither of them even glanced his way.

Faintly all around him, he could hear pounding and mechanical noises and the mostly incomprehensible babbling from the PA system, sounds that were part of life on the *Deepwater Venture,* a semi-submersible oil platform fifty-seven miles off the coast of Texas.

His mother chattered on, naming off more charming young women she knew, more of the still single daughters of her endless list of women friends. He was starting to think he would just have to back out of the Thanksgiving visit, to tell her he wasn't going to be able to make it home after all.

Sorry, Mom. Something big has come up, something really big. I just can't be there....

But then he heard swearing. And the swift pounding of heavy boots on the stairs. The sounds were coming closer, descending on him from the deck above.

He knew the voice: Sam Jaworski, the rig manager in charge of the drilling department—aka the tool pusher. Sam was one of eight women on the rig. The safety officer was also a woman. And the rest worked in food service or housekeeping.

Sam, in coveralls, safety glasses and a hard hat, stomped into the lounge at full volume. She was on a roll with nonstop, semi-dirty, surprisingly imaginative language.

His mother was *still* talking. "So you see, I have found several fun, smart, attractive girls you'll get a chance to meet."

Sam sent him a quick acknowledging glance. He raised a hand in greeting. She gave the roughnecks a wave and then clomped over to the coffee machine. She poured herself a cup. There was a patch sewn on the right butt cheek of her coveralls. It read I Ain't Yo' Mama. She had to stop swearing to take a big swig of coffee.

But as soon as she swallowed, she was at it again. "And then dunk his sorry, skinny ass in a burnin' barrel of bubbling black crude…"

Travis grinned for the first time since he'd picked up the phone to call his mom. Sam's swearing was always more enthusiastic than obscene. And it never failed to make him smile.

And then he said, without even stopping to consider the possible consequences, "Mom, I already have a girl." He held back a chuckle. *Well, sort of a girl.*

Sam took off her hard hat and safety glasses, turned toward him and propped a hip against the counter. She slurped up a big sip of coffee—and swore some more.

On the other end of the line, his mom let out a delighted trill of laughter. "Travis, how wonderful. Why didn't you say so?"

"Well, Mom, you haven't exactly let me get a word in edgewise."

"Oh, honey." She was instantly regretful. "I'm sorry. I was just so glad to hear from you. And I wanted to…

Well, it doesn't matter now. Forgive me for being a poor listener?"

"You know I do."

She asked eagerly, "What's her name? Do I know her?"

More choice expletives from Sam. He turned to the wall, cupped his hand around the mouthpiece of the phone, and told his mother, "Samantha, Mom. Samantha Jaworski—and no, you don't."

His mother made a thoughtful sound. "But you've mentioned her often, haven't you, over the years?"

"Yeah, Mom. I've mentioned her." He'd known Sam for more than a decade now.

"And she's nice, isn't she? You two have been friends for a long time, as I recall."

"Yeah, we have. And she's…she's lovely." He slanted a glance at Sam as she sniffed and rubbed her nose with the back of her grease-smeared hand. "Very delicate."

Sam stood six feet tall and she was stronger than most men. She had to be, to get where she'd gotten in the oil business. Most tool pushers were older than she was. And male.

On a rig, the buck stopped at the tool pusher. Sam was on the drilling-contractor payroll. She did everything from making sure work schedules were met to setting up machines and equipment. She prepared production reports. She recommended hirings and firings and decided who was ready for promotion. She supervised and she coordinated. She trained workers in their duties and in safety procedures. She requisitioned materials and supplies. And if it came right down to it, she could haul and connect pipe with the best of them.

On this job, Travis had had the pleasure of working closely with her. He was the company man, paid to

represent the interests of the oil company South Texas
Oil Industries. Some pushers didn't get along with the
company man. They didn't like being answerable to
the exploration and operation end of the business. Sam
didn't have that problem. She not only had her men's
respect, but she also worked well with others.

She was an amazing woman, Sam Jaworski. But delicate?

Not in the least.

"I get it now," his mother said. "I've been chattering
away and the whole time you've been trying to tell me
that you're bringing her to Thanksgiving, to the reaffirmation of our vows."

Crap. He should have seen that coming. Suddenly,
his little private joke took on scary ramifications. "Uh,
well…"

"Honey, I understand how it's been for you." She
didn't, not really. But he knew she meant well. She kept
on, "You've been…hurt and let down before. I can see
where you might be afraid to let it get serious with Samantha. But that's all right. Just ask her to come with
you. Just take that step."

"Well, I…" He stalled some more, grasping for the
right words, the magic words that would get his mother
off his back about this once and for all. Those words
didn't come. "Mom, really, I don't think that's a good
idea."

"Why not?"

"I just don't, okay?"

His mom finally gave it up. "All right, if you don't
want to invite her, if your relationship hasn't gotten to
that point yet, well, all right." She sighed. And then she
brightened and teased, "At least Cybil and LouJo and
Ashley will be happy to know they still have a chance."

Trapped. His gut churned and his pulse pounded. And then he heard himself say, "As a matter of fact, Sam and I are engaged."

It just kind of popped out. He blinked at the wall. Had he really said that?

His mother cried out in joy. "Travis, how wonderful! I can't believe you didn't tell me until now."

Had Sam heard him say that? He sent the tall, broad-shouldered woman in the grease-streaked coveralls another furtive glance. Uh-uh. She'd turned back to the sink to wash her hands. As he faced the wall once more, he heard her rip a paper towel off the roll.

He looked again. Clomp, clomp, clomp. Coffee mug in hand, she sauntered over to the nearer TV and grabbed the remote. The screen came alive and she started channel surfing.

Meanwhile, on the other end of the line, his mother was on the case. "And that settles it. You must bring her with you. I won't take no for an answer, not now."

He stared at Sam's I Ain't Yo' Mama backside, at her short brown hair, creased tight to her skull from the hard hat's inner band, at her big steel-toed boots. Had he lost his mind? There was no win in lying to his mom—especially not about being engaged. "Uh, well..."

"Please, Travis, invite her. I'm so happy for you. And you know we're all going to want to meet her."

"Mom, I—"

"Please." Her voice was so gentle. And hopeful. And maybe even somewhat sad—as though she knew that in the end, he was going to disappoint her, that Sam would not be coming with him, no matter what his mother said to encourage him to bring her.

Now he felt like a complete jerk. For lying about

Sam. For disappointing his mom. For everything. "Look, Mom. I'll...check with Sam, okay?"

Dear God in heaven. Where had *that* come from? Bad, bad idea.

"Oh, Travis." His mom was suddenly sounding happy again. "That's wonderful. We'll be expecting both of you, then."

What the hell? "Uh, no. Wait, really. You can't start expecting anything. I said I would *ask* her."

"And I just know she'll say yes. Two weeks from today, as planned. Love you. Bye now."

"Mom. I mean it. Don't... Wait! I..." But it was no good. She'd already hung up.

He took the phone away from his ear and gave it a dirty look. Then he started to call her back—but stopped in mid-dial.

Why ask for more trouble? Hadn't he gotten himself plenty already?

Grumbling under his breath, he snagged the phone back onto the wall mount, yanked out a chair at the table a few feet away and dropped into it.

Sam had been waiting for Travis to finish on the phone. She watched as the two roughnecks wrapped up their bowling game and went back up the stairs.

Good. She didn't need anyone listening in.

She heard Travis hang up, and then the sound of a chair scraping the floor as he pulled it out from the table. She switched off the TV and turned to him. "That roustabout Jimmy Betts? Born without a brain. A walking safety hazard. Give that boy a length of pipe and someone is bound to get whacked in the frickin' head."

He seemed distracted, slumped in the chair, a frown

on his handsome face. But after a second or two, he said, "He'll learn. They all do—or they don't last."

Sam let a snort do for a reply to that. And then she tossed down the remote and went to join him. She plunked her coffee on the table, swung a chair around and straddled it backward. Stacking her arms on the chair back, she leaned her chin on them. She studied him. He stared back at her, but his brown eyes still had a faraway look in them.

"Your mama, huh?" she finally asked. "Driving you crazy again?"

He grunted. "That's right."

"She still trying to find you the new love of your life?"

He grunted a second time and looked at her kind of strangely. She got the message. He wasn't in the mood to talk about his mother and her plans to get him hog-tied and branded.

Sam could read Travis pretty well. After all, they'd been friends since way back when he was nineteen and she was eighteen. Back then, Travis had worked on the oil well at her dad's South Dakota ranch.

So, all right. Not talking about his mother was fine with her. She had something else on her mind anyway.

Sam indulged in a glum look around the lounge. It was a large room. But the low ceiling, the absence of windows and the fluorescent lighting gave the space a sort of subterranean glow. It made Travis look tired, turned his tanned skin kind of pasty. She didn't even want to think about how it made *her* look.

Travis's dark brows drew together. "Got something on your mind, Sam?"

Oh, yes, she did. "You have no idea how frickin' tired

I am of being on this rig. And I could seriously use a tall cold one about now, you know?"

They grunted in unison then. There was no liquor allowed on the rig.

Most rig workers had the usual two-weeks-on, two-weeks-off rotation. Not the pusher. Sam had been on the rig for over a month now, working twelve-hour shifts seven days a week. A week more and she would be back on land at last. She could not wait. And the rock docs—the engineers—were saying that the four-month drilling process was within days of completion. Her job on the *Deepwater Venture* was ending anyway. She wouldn't be signing on to another rig to start all over again.

"Travis, I've been thinking…"

He waited, watching her.

She sat straighter and swept both arms wide, a gesture meant to include not only the lounge, but every inch of the semi-submersible rig, from the operating deck and the cranes and derrick soaring above it, to the ballasted, watertight pontoons below the ocean's surface that held the giant platform afloat. "I used to love the challenge, you know? Doing a man's job and doing it right. Earning and keeping the men's respect—in spite of being female, even though I was younger than half of them. But lately, well, I'm thinking it's time to change it up a little. I'm thirty years old. It's a time when a person can start to wonder about things."

He tipped his head to the side, frowning. "What things?"

"Things like getting back to the real world, like living on solid ground full-time, like…I don't know, letting my hair grow, for cryin' out loud, getting a job where I don't end up covered in drilling mud and grease at least once a shift. Sitting in an employee lounge that has actual windows—windows that look out on something other than water and more water."

He made a low noise. Was it a doubtful kind of sound? What? He didn't think she could make it in a desk job?

She scowled at him and raked her fingers back through her sweaty, chopped-off hair. "And you can just stop looking at me like that, Travis Bravo. Yeah, I know what working in an office is going to mean. I get that I'm going to have to clean up my language and maybe even learn to wear a damn dress now and then. And I'm ready for that."

He kept on looking at her. Studying her, really. What the hell was he thinking?

She threw out both arms again, glanced left and then right—and then directly at him again. *"What?"* she demanded.

He swung his boots up onto the molded plastic chair next to his. Way too casually, he suggested, "So, Sam. Want to come to my parents' wedding?"

Okay, now she was totally lost. "Your parents' *wedding?* Didn't that already happen? Y'know like, oh, a hundred years ago? Travis, I have no idea what you're talking about."

One corner of his mouth quirked up. "Well, okay. Technically, it's a reaffirmation of their wedding vows. It's happening out at Bravo Ridge." He'd spoken of Bravo Ridge often. It was his family's ranch near San Antonio. "It'll be on Thanksgiving Day."

She sat back and folded her arms across her middle. She'd always wondered about his family, the high-class, powerful San Antonio Bravos. It would be interesting to meet them all, to match the real, flesh-and-blood people to the faces in the pictures Travis had shown her over the years.

Then again, maybe not. "I don't think so...."

"Come on. Why not?"

"Well, to be honest, from everything you've said about your family, I don't think I'd fit in with them."

"Sure you will."

"I don't *even* have the clothes for something like that, let alone the manners. And I don't have any fancy pedigree, either. I'd probably embarrass you."

"You could never embarrass me. You're the best. And what do you mean, pedigree? It's America. We're all equal, remember? And if you're nervous about your clothes, I'll deal with that."

She looked at him sideways. "How, exactly are *you* going deal with *my* clothes?"

"I'll buy you some new ones."

"No way. I buy my own stuff. But even if I maxed out my credit cards getting a whole new wardrobe, well, I still wouldn't know which frickin' fork to use."

He swung his feet to the floor and canted toward her in the chair. "So we'll get you a coach. A few days in Houston beforehand should do it."

"Um. Travis, I'm not really understanding what exactly you're up to here."

"I just said. You'll have time. A whole week to get ready after you're back on land, plenty of time to buy the clothes and work with the coach."

"The coach," she repeated blankly.

"Yeah, the coach. Someone who's an expert on all that stuff—on the clothes, the makeup, the...use of the silverware, whatever. By the time you meet my mom, you'll be more than ready."

"More than ready for...?"

"Everything." He smiled. It wasn't a very sincere smile.

She rubbed her temples with the tips of her fingers. Really, he was making her head spin. "Travis, cut the crap. What *exactly* are you trying to talk me into?"

He glanced away, and then back. "Before I get too specific, I just want to know you'll keep an open mind about the whole thing, okay?"

"Yeah, well. Before I can keep an open mind, I need to know what I'm supposed to be keeping an open mind about."

He hoisted his feet back up on the chair again. "It's like this. I want you to help me get my mom off my back."

She followed. Kind of. "You mean about all the, er, *suitable* young women, right?"

He nodded. "I need you to be my date—for a week, including Thanksgiving."

"You think if you bring a date, your mom will stop trying to fix you up?"

He pulled a face and scratched the back of his head. "Well, yeah. For a while. If my date was…more than just a date."

"What do you mean, more than just a frickin' date?"

"Okay, it's like this. I want you to pretend that you're my fiancée."

Travis didn't find the look on Sam's face the least bit encouraging.

She swore. Colorfully. And then she jumped up from the chair, strode around the table to him—and slapped him upside the back of the head.

He shoved her hand away. "Ouch! Knock it off."

She gave a disgusted snort. "Have you lost your mind?"

He put up both hands to back her off. "Look. It just… slipped out when I was talking to her, okay?"

"It? What?"

"She was all over me, pressuring me, going down the list of all the women she wants me to meet. And then you came down from the deck and I, well, all of a sudden, I was saying I already had a girl. I said *you* were my girl and we were engaged."

Sam did more swearing. And then she returned to her chair, grabbed the back of it, spun it around and sat down in it front ways that time. "What *have* you been smoking?"

"Not a thing. You know that. And can you just think it over? Please? Don't say no without giving it some serious consideration. You get the coach and the clothes to help you change up your life. And I have a few strings I can pull, too, for you. To make sure you get the job you want."

She had her arms folded good and tight across her middle by then. "There's just one teensy problem."

"What?"

"It's a big wonkin' lie."

"I know that, but it can't be helped."

"Sure, it can. Call your mom back. Tell her you lied and I'm not your girl after all. And when you want a girl, you'll find her yourself."

"Sam, come on…"

She pressed her lips together, blew out a breath—and flipped him the bird.

But he refused to give up. The more he thought about it, the more this looked like a solution to his problem.

A temporary solution, yeah. But still. Even temporary was better than no solution at all.

"Look," he said. "You do this for me, I figure it's good for up to a year of peace and quiet on my mother's part."

"Why don't you just *talk* to your mother? Tell her how you feel, tell her you want her to back off and mind her own business."

"You think I haven't? It doesn't matter what I say, she thinks she's doing the right thing for me. She thinks it's for my own good. And when my mother thinks what she's doing is for the good of one of her children, there's no stopping her. There's no getting her to see the light and admit that she's got it all wrong."

"But making up some big old lie is not the answer. It's…just not you. You're a straight-ahead guy. No frills and no fancy footwork. I've always liked that about you."

He laid it right out for her. "Sam, I'm desperate. I need a break from this garbage. I need to be able to go home for once without having a bunch of sweet-faced Texas debutantes in their best party dresses lined up waiting to meet me. I need to be able to call my mom without being beat over the head with all the women she wants to introduce me to."

"Maybe if you just gave it a chance with one of them, you'd find out that—"

"Stop. Don't go there. You know I'm not up for that. I *had* the love of my life. She died. And I already tried it with the woman who could never take her place."

"But it's been years and years since you lost Rachel. And just because it didn't work out with Wanda doesn't mean there isn't someone else out there who's right for you."

He gave her a really dirty look, and then he glanced away. "You're starting to sound like my mother. I don't need that."

"Travis, I only—"

He turned to meet her eyes again. "Help me out, Sam. Help me out and I'll help *you* out. Win-win. You'll see. You can have the new life you've been dreaming of. All you have to do to get it is a little favor for a friend."

Chapter Two

A week and a day later, Sam entered the lobby of Houston's Four Seasons Hotel.

She wore a gray pantsuit with a white blouse and black flats. Not exactly glamorous. But hey. At least it was something other than coveralls, steel-toed boots and a hard hat.

Unfortunately, her hair was being really annoying that day. It was only an inch long, for cripes' sake. But still, it insisted on curling every which way.

Her makeup? She wore none—and not because she hadn't tried. Three times, she'd applied blush, lip gloss and mascara. She'd picked those up the day before at Walmart in an effort to look more pulled-together for this big adventure she probably shouldn't have let herself be talked into in the first place. Each time she put the makeup on, she'd had to scrub it right off again. It just didn't look right on her. So in the end, she decided to go without.

The Four Seasons was about the fanciest hotel in Houston. She'd expected old-fashioned elegance. But the lobby was modern. The furniture had clean, trendy lines. The carpets were in black-and-white geometric patterns. There was also bright color—in the modern art on the walls, in the purple pillows, all plump and inviting on the tan and off-white sofas.

And where the hell was Travis, anyway? He'd promised he would be here waiting for her.

She tried not to gape like the oversize hayseed she knew herself to be. She told herself it was all in her mind that the bellmen and concierge clerks were staring at her and wondering what she was doing there. What did a concierge clerk care if she was as big as a horse and every bit as muscular? So what if she looked more manly than most of the guys in the place? She had as much right to be there as anyone else.

And she did have her pride. Chin up, her black leather tote hooked on a shoulder, she sauntered past the check-in desk and chose a sofa thick with bright pillows beneath a giant circular chandelier dripping with about a hundred thousand crystals.

When she reached the sofa, she turned and lowered herself into it with care. She kept her knees together, her black flats planted on the thick carpet, neatly, side-by-side. Easing the tote off her shoulder, she put it at her feet. And then, sitting very still and very straight, she folded her hands in her lap and she waited.

She tried not to squirm, tried to keep her face calm and composed. The minutes crawled by.

Travis, you SOB, where are you?

He'd better get there damn soon or she wouldn't be waiting when he finally did arrive. She pressed her lips together, swallowed, felt the nervous sweat beginning to seep through the underarms of her new shirt.

Wasn't there some old saying about how a person should beware of all situations that require new clothes?

Uh, yeah. Exactly.

Travis, unless you show up right this minute, I am going to get up and walk out of here. And then, the next time I see you, I will beat the ever lovin' crap out of you....

"Sam. Great. There you are...."

So. He was there. At last.

Sam let out the breath she hadn't realized she was holding. Turning to look over her shoulder, she watched him striding toward her, wearing really nice black jeans and a sport jacket, looking like he owned the place. With him was a short, skinny man in a striped shirt with a big white collar, linen pants and suspenders. The man's thick, wavy blond hair was bigger than he was. Sam could have picked him up with one hand, tucked him under her arm and carried him several city blocks without even breathing hard.

She snatched up her tote and rose to meet them.

"Lookin' good," said Travis. He grabbed her in a quick hug. When he let her go, he turned to the tiny, bird-boned guy with the big hair. "Jonathan, Sam. Sam, Jonathan."

The little guy gave her the once-over through eyes as small and bright and birdlike as the rest of him. "Hello, Samantha. I can see we've got our work cut out for us."

Her coach. Of course. Pretentious frickin' twit. She started to say something to put him in his place, but then changed her mind. He might be pretentious, but then again, he was also right. No point in beating up the messenger. She had a lot to learn if she wanted a different kind of life. "Yeah," she said drily. "I hope you're up to the job."

Travis said, "I found him on the internet. And I'm betting he's the best."

Jonathan tossed his big hair. "No time to waste, is there? Shall we go up?"

The suite was spectacular. All in relaxing colors— dusty greens and creamy tans and warm golds, with a great view of downtown Houston. Two bedrooms. One for her, one for her coach.

Travis had his town house in the city.

She stood at the window and looked out at the sky-line and worried about how much this had to be cost-ing him.

He came to stand with her. "Great view, huh?"

"Yeah. Where's Jonathan?" she asked the question low, out of the corner of her mouth.

"He's in his room, getting settled."

She decided to go ahead and ask him about the ex-pense. "This all looks…really pricey, Travis."

"That's right." He sounded so pleased with himself. "Didn't I promise you a crash course in how the other half lives?"

"I'm just saying it's enough that you hired me my own personal coach. That had to cost plenty. And then the clothes. That'll be plenty more. You really didn't need to spring for a suite at the Four Seasons."

He put an arm around her shoulder, gave it a reassur-ing squeeze. "Only the best for my favorite fiancée."

She eased out from under his hold. "You're blowing me off."

"No, I'm not."

"It just, you know, seems like it's kind of overkill.

Way too frickin' expensive overkill. I mean, I know you have your investments and all, but I hate to see you waste your hard-earned money."

"Stop worrying—and anyway, I didn't raid my portfolio for this." He leaned in closer and lowered his voice to a soft growl. "Did I ever tell you about my giant trust fund?"

"You did, but you always said—"

"—that I would never touch it. And I haven't. Not once. Until now."

She turned to him, met his kind dark eyes. "You broke into your trust fund for *this?*"

He gave her an easy smile. "About time, I was thinking—and no, I didn't *break* into it. It's mine, after all, just sitting there, waiting for me, the prodigal son, to finally take advantage of what being a Bravo has always offered me."

She smiled too, then. "The prodigal son. I never thought of you that way. And I thought a prodigal was a wild-living big spender."

"I was thinking more in the sense of the son who left home."

"Well, you are that."

"And my mom only wants me to come home."

"And get married to a nice Texas debutante…"

"Lucky for me, I have you to save me from that."

She had the strangest desire to lay her hand along the side of his smooth, freshly shaved cheek. But that seemed uncalled-for. They weren't pretending to be engaged *yet,* after all. "Yeah, well," she said vaguely. "We'll see…."

"Ahem." It was Jonathan. He stood over by the sitting area, holding a laptop against his narrow chest. He set the laptop on the gleaming glass surface of the coffee table and then clapped his skinny hands together. "All right, then. Let's begin." He sat down on the sofa and patted the cushion next to him. "Samantha, come and sit by me." She sent Travis a what-have-you-gotten-me-into glance and then went over and sat next to Jonathan, who signaled to Travis with a dramatic flourish. "You, too. Have a seat." Travis claimed a wing chair across the coffee table.

Sam was realizing that she found her new coach kind of amusing. She liked his take-charge attitude and self-assurance. He might be little, but every sentence, every gesture, was delivered on a grand scale. "So, Jonathan, what's your last name?"

He turned slowly to look up at her, one pencil-thin eyebrow raised. "Just Jonathan, darling."

Oh, wow. Now she was his darling. She chuckled. "Well, all right."

Travis got up and went to grab an apple from the basket on the granite wet bar. "I flew Jonathan in from L.A. And before I did, I checked out his references. He comes highly recommended." He bit a big, crunchy hunk out of the apple.

Jonathan almost smiled—or at least the corners of his tiny mouth lifted a fraction. "I have my own cable show," he said proudly. *"Jeer-worthy to Cheer-worthy."* He opened the laptop and fiddled with the keyboard for a moment. His picture appeared on the screen. He sat in a plush leather chair in a red-walled room, his hair bigger and wavier than it was in person. A bookcase behind him was filled with gold-tooled leather volumes and accented with what seemed to be valuable antiques. "My website," he said. She'd already figured that out, of course, from the ornate gold header at the top of the page. "JustJonathan.com."

"Uh. Real nice," she said.

"Thank you, darling." He clicked the mouse. A really sad-looking redhead appeared on the screen. Ruddy skin, frizzy hair, a face as round as a dinner plate. "Amanda Richly. Before." *Click.* "And after," he said proudly.

The second image was the same redhead. But the same redhead, transformed. Now her hair was thick and wavy and completely unfrizzed, her skin pink and perfect, her blue eyes framed by long, lush red-brown lashes. She was no longer sad. In fact, her happy smile brought out the cute dimples in her cheeks.

"Wow. Way to go, Jonathan." Sam elbowed him in his itty-bitty ribs.

He almost fell over sideways. But not quite. "Please don't hurt me, darling," he said drily. She laughed. And then he preened, "Trust me. I know what I'm doing."

"I can see that." She shared a nod with Travis, who remained by the wet bar, polishing off his apple.

Jonathan clicked through several more transformations. Each one was amazing. Sam was impressed and she told Jonathan so.

Finally, he snapped the laptop shut and frowned at her. "If we are to work together, I need to be able to be perfectly frank."

"Go for it." She braced herself for the bad news.

"You're a disaster, my sweet." He caught her hands, turned them over, gave a small gasp of pure distress. "Look at these. What have you been doing with them, scraping barnacles off a ship's hull?"

"Close," she confessed.

He shook his head. "Never mind. Don't tell me. I don't need specifics." He turned her hands over again, set them on her knees, and patted the backs of them.

Next, scowling, he touched her hair. And then he caught her face between his soft, warm palms. "We must get you to the spa immediately," he announced. "You will need *everything*. It's going to take a while. And the peels, the scrubs, the masks and the mud wraps, the hair, nails and makeup are only the beginning. There will be shopping. Intensive, goal-centered shopping. I will go with you, of course, give you guidance, save you from yourself should you try and buy another unfortunate pantsuit."

She winced and looked down at the pantsuit in question. "Unfortunate? I bought it yesterday. I know it's not great. But I thought it was better than just unfortunate."

He wiggled a finger at her. "Remember. Absolute honesty."

"Yeah. All right. Hit me with it."

He caught the fabric of her sleeve, fingered it and shuddered. "You must learn to buy clothing made from natural fibers, my love. It not only looks so much better, but it also lets the skin breathe and doesn't trap odors."

"Odors," she echoed weakly, way too aware of the lingering dampness beneath her arms.

"I noticed you had just that big black bag."

She shrugged. "Well, I only brought a couple of changes of underwear and some pj's. I thought we would be buying the rest."

"Very good. Excellent. Out with the old and all things polyester. And in with the new. By the time I'm through with you, you won't be afraid of five-inch Manolo Blahniks, or a little color."

She wasn't a complete idiot. She knew who Manolo Blahnik was. She'd watched a few episodes of *Sex and the City* back in the day. "Uh, Jonathan. Maybe you didn't notice. I don't wear high heels because I'm already taller than just about everyone else."

"Yes, you are. And your height is spectacular."

Travis folded his big frame back into the wing chair. He was grinning. "Yep. Absolutely spectacular."

She blinked at him. "Uh. It is?"

Jonathan patted her arm. "You also have excellent bone structure. Fabulous cheekbones."

Her sagging spirits lifted. She pressed her fingers to the cheekbones in question. "Well, that's good."

"And I can see you are in prime physical condition. We can use that."

"Er...we can?"

"Oh, yes. Gone are the days when a pretty woman had to be tiny and delicate. It's okay at last to be a woman of substance. Muscles, wide shoulders, strong calves and hard thighs are the height of fashion now."

Maybe it wasn't as bad as she'd thought. She dared to grin.

Jonathan frowned, shook his head and then smoothed his acres of hair carefully back into place. "Don't become overconfident, my love. You've got a lot to learn. And a limited amount of time to do it in."

At Jonathan's request, Travis got up to go a few minutes later.

"You will not see Samantha until Saturday evening," her coach announced in what Samantha considered a very grim tone. "For the final test."

"Test?" Sam piped up weakly.

"Don't ask." Jonathan remained deadly serious. "Not yet. We are only beginning. And there's a long way to go before we're ready to discuss the final test."

Travis gave her a hug at the door. That was the second time he'd hugged her that day—first, in the lobby, now here, as he was leaving. As a rule, she and Travis didn't hug much. Especially the past few months when they'd been working on the rig together. Hugs would not be professional.

But now, with his strong arms around her, she realized how much she enjoyed getting the chance to lean on him. He was a couple of inches taller than she was, and even broader in the shoulders and deeper in the chest. It felt good to hug him. She knew she could hug him hard and never hurt him. For a girl of her size and strength, that was a rare thing.

He took her by the shoulders and held her away from him so he could meet her eyes. "You going to be okay?"

She nodded and forced a smile for him. "Go on. I'll be fine." She stepped back from the comforting circle of his hold. He opened the door and went through it.

Instantly she wanted to reach out and grab him back. She'd always found his presence reassuring—and she could really use some reassurance about now. She took a step out into the hallway and watched him stride confidently toward the elevators.

It was kind of funny, really. She risked her life just about daily on the job. An oil rig, after all, was a pretty dangerous place. But she'd never been as scared as she was right then, in that hotel suite, watching Travis walk away from her. The very idea of having to learn to get her girly on freaked her the hell out. It would be easier if Travis could stay.

"Shut the door, Samantha." Jonathan's voice was almost tender.

She stepped back into the room and did what he told her to. And then she leaned her forehead against that door and thought about what a good friend Travis had been to her over the years.

At the end of the first year of their friendship, just before she turned nineteen, he'd helped her get her start in the oil business. He'd spoken up for her when she tried for her first job as a roustabout on a land rig. They didn't want to hire her because she was a woman and what woman could hold up under the grueling physical labor that would be required of her?

Thanks to Travis, she got that job, as what they called a "worm," the lowest of the low in the rig pecking order. She got that job and she kept up with the men. She did it all. She hauled pipe and dug trenches, cleaned up mud and oil and whatever else got all over the equipment. She cleaned threads, scraped and painted the various rig components. She worked her ass off and she never shirked.

That first job was where she'd met a certain rough-neck, Zachary Gunn. She'd fallen in love with Zach—fallen in love for the first and only time in her life. And when Zach turned out to be a rotten, no-good bigmouth jerk who told everyone what he'd done with her and that she'd been really bad at it, Travis was there.

Travis beat the ever-lovin' you-know-what out of that sorry SOB. And then kicked him off the rig.

As a rule, Sam fought her own battles. But that one time, it meant more than she could ever say to know that Travis Bravo had her back.

"Time to get started," said Jonathan. "Tell me you're ready."

Sam straightened her spine and turned to face her coach. "I'm ready. Let's go."

Chapter Three

That first day was really bad.

Before they did anything, Jonathan took a bunch of pictures of her from different angles, pictures of her standing, pictures of her sitting. Pictures from the front, the back, the side. Full-length pictures and also close-up ones.

She knew what those pictures were: the "before" pictures. She knew they were awful.

And she sincerely hoped that the "afters," days from now, would be a whole lot better.

Once Jonathan decided he had enough ugly shots of her, he had her sign a paper giving him permission to use the pictures on his website. And then he took her to the hotel spa.

It was a nice place. Sam loved that it was simple, not froufrou or frilly in the least. It was soothing just to be there.

Until the torture started.

Jonathan said her skin needed all the help it could get. There was deep-tissue cleaning and a chemical peel. There was hot mud wrapped all around her in steaming wet towels. There was waxing—of her legs and under her arms. The bikini wax was the worst.

She'd rather take a bath in drilling mud than get that done again.

Jonathan laughed when she told him that. "You'll get waxed, darling. And regularly. A woman should be sleek. Smooth. Excess body hair is not the least bit feminine."

She grunted. "Gee, Jonathan. Thanks a bunch for sharing."

There was massage. That wasn't so bad.

But after that, there was the manicure and the pedicure. Those went on forever and involved soaking and exfoliating and scrubbing at every callous and rough spot, of which there were many.

Hours later, when they were finished with her for the day, her face was lobster-red from the peel and they'd given her booties and white gloves. She had to slather on this gooey ointment before bed nightly, they had told her at the spa, both on her hands and her feet, and then wear the gloves and booties to bed every night for the whole week.

She was starving by the time she got back to the suite. She wanted a burger and fries and a strawberry shake. Or at least a big slab of meatloaf and a mountain of mashed potatoes with a healthy side of mushy canned green beans. On the rig, the kitchen was open round-the-clock and you could get yourself a huge pile of hot food—heavy on the starches and fats and red meat—any time you got the least bit hungry.

Not here, though. Jonathan ordered room service for them.

When it came, she wanted to break down and cry. All day being waxed and plucked and pummeled in the spa. And for dinner, she got an itsy-bitsy mound of barely cooked broccoli, three tiny red potatoes. And grilled salmon.

Actually, it was delicious. But it wasn't enough to keep a fly alive.

She begged for more. Jonathan refused to let her even have one more dinky red potato. He said she wasn't getting enough exercise to eat the way she was apparently accustomed to eating.

It was too much. She yelled at him. "Jonathan, I would be frickin' happy to exercise. I'll go down to the gym right this minute and bench-press my butt off if you will only swear on your life that there'll be a blood-rare T-bone and a baked potato slathered in butter and sour cream waiting for me when I get back up here to this frickin' tasteful, so-classy suite."

He only shook his head. He was a slave driver, that Jonathan.

After the piddly-ass meal, they had grammar lessons. He made her take a vow that she would never use the word *frickin'* again in this lifetime. And then he tutored her on how to eat at a table set with endless pieces of unrecognizable silverware.

It was actually pretty simple, once he explained that you started with the outermost fork or knife or spoon and worked your way in. And if in doubt, you waited to pick up the next tong or cracker or pointy lobster-picking thing until you were able to subtly observe what your host or hostess did with it.

"Subt-ly," Jonathan repeated, making a big deal

of both syllables. "And by 'subtly,' I mean a sideways glance in the direction of the hostess in question. No open-mouthed ogling. One must learn, darling, to accomplish one's goal in such a way as not to telegraph one's ignorance to the table at large."

"Gotcha," she answered, feeling vaguely resentful. Yeah, okay. She did have a lot to learn, but she'd never been the kind to stare with her mouth open.

He sighed in a way that indicated she caused him endless emotional pain. "*Gotcha.* Another word you would do well to remove from your vocabulary."

"Jonathan, you keep on like this, I won't have any *frick*—er, darn words left."

"But, darling, you will learn new ones. I will see to that—and as concerns your elbows…"

"Yeah, what about 'em?" She pushed back her sleeve. "They've been creamed and scrubbed and buffed just about down to the bone."

"Yes, they do *look* much better."

"Thanks, but that's not what I was getting at."

"It doesn't matter what *you're* getting at. You're the student. You're here to watch, listen and learn. And as to elbows, they are under no circumstances to be allowed on the surface of the table while one is still indulging in the meal. Understood?"

"Yeah, I knew that." Not that she'd ever cared all that much where she put her elbows while she was eating. But still. Everybody knew they weren't supposed to be on the table, even if most people didn't give a damn either way.

"However." There was a definite gleam in Jonathan's beady little eyes. "*After* the meal, while one lingers, chatting, enjoying the heady conversation that so often swirls around the table when one is in good company…

then, and only then, is it considered acceptable to delicately brace one, or even both elbows on the tablecloth."

She couldn't help grinning. "Delicately, huh?"

"Yes, well. We'll have to work on that."

After the lessons on which piece of silverware to use when, they moved on to her clothing. He said they would try some preliminary shopping tomorrow. He wanted her to think about what colors would work on her—bright, vivid jewel colors, he said. "And some neutrals. But. No. Gray. Ever." He made each word a sentence. And then he elaborated. "Gray does nothing for your coloring, Samantha. Less than nothing. Gray makes you look embalmed."

"Gee. Good to know."

"Sarcasm is not appreciated."

"I'll keep that in mind, Jonathan—if you will."

There was more lecturing on the subject of natural fibers. She would wear cotton, silk, linen and wool. And *only* cotton, silk, linen and wool. "And no frills. We'll go for simplicity with you. And some drama. But nothing fluffy or ruffled. Nothing too…precious. Because, darling, you are not the precious type."

Of course, he had examples to show her on his laptop. She thought he was absolutely right in his judgment of what should work well for her clothing-wise, so she didn't give him too much of a hard time during the wardrobe lesson. She listened and did her best to absorb what he taught her.

At nine-thirty that evening, she was allowed a cup of tea and an orange. He admonished her to hold her teacup just so, to sip without slurping—and never to chew with her mouth open.

Somehow, he inspired the brat in her. She longed to open her mouth good and wide and stick out her tongue at him *before* swallowing the section of orange she'd been so cautiously, *delicately* munching.

But she didn't. She kept her mouth shut and she swallowed the orange and she sipped without slurping at her unsweetened tea.

He gave her a book to read when he sent her to bed: *Miss Manners' Guide to the Turn-of-the-Millennium*. She turned the pages with white-gloved fingers because both of her hands were greased up and encased in the special gloves they'd given her at the spa.

She even laughed now and then. Miss Manners was funny. And most of her advice made sense really.

Once you got past the strange realization that the way Miss Manners used words was almost identical to the way Jonathan talked.

The next day was worse.

It was the shopping. She hated it.

She'd really thought she had a pretty good idea of the clothing rules Jonathan had drilled into her the evening before. But it wasn't the same, being out there in some fancy, expensive department store, trying to choose something vivid in color with nice, simple lines—in cotton, linen, silk or wool—when there were racks and racks packed with skirts and blouses and dresses and every other damn thing you ever might consider wanting to wear.

It made her feel sick to her stomach. Suddenly she was longing to be back on the rig, wearing her boots and coveralls, slathered in drilling mud, hitting the deck as Jimmy Betts swung a length of pipe in her direction.

Plus she was starving. *Frickin'* starving, as a matter of fact—and no, she didn't say the forbidden word out loud.

But boy, was she tempted to.

She needed a decent meal and she needed to *not* have to shop anymore.

But Jonathan was relentless. He wouldn't let her go back to the hotel.

At noon, he took her to some prissy, ferny downtown lunch place. And he ordered her a salad and an iced tea with lemon. She wanted to kill him. She truly did. Just snap his tiny twig of a neck between her two big hands.

But then she reminded herself that she was going to do this. She was sticking out this ridiculous crash course in being a suitable pretend fiancée for Aleta Bravo's precious prodigal son. She *needed* this, and she knew it. She wanted a chance at a new life.

And if being waxed and peeled and plucked and starved half to death, if having to shop all day and all night until she finally managed to find something simple and bright in a natural fabric—if getting *trained* in how to sip tea and sit down at a table with rich people…

If all that had to be done for her to get a fresh start, well, fine. She would do it. She would not give up.

She was made of tougher stuff than that.

So she ate her salad, slowly. Calmly. In small bites, chewing with her mouth shut. She sipped her iced tea.

And then they shopped some more.

It didn't get easier.

In the end, after hours and hours of lurking twenty feet away, watching her *subtly* out of the corner of his eye, Jonathan came to her rescue. He started choosing things for her to try on.

Loaded down with shopping bags, they got back to the hotel at six-thirty. Sam now had five new dresses, six pairs of incredibly expensive shoes, four sweaters, three shirts, two pairs of designer jeans…and more. Much more.

Jonathan had chosen everything. His taste was just disgustingly great. Even with her chopped-off hair and no makeup and her face still red from yesterday's peel— she wasn't getting the hair or the makeup until near the end of her training, he had told her—she could see the difference the right clothes made.

At the hotel, he ordered quail for dinner—two of them each. Two tiny plump birds with a side of slivered carrots, which were drizzled in some heavenly sauce. She wanted to fall on those dinky birds and shove them, whole, into her wide-open mouth. She wanted to devour them, itty-bitty bones and all.

But she waited, hands and napkin in her lap, for his instructions.

He surprised her. "One eats quail with one's hands," Jonathan said. "Some foods are simply too small, or too bony, to be eaten any other way. In fact, the bones themselves are quite delicate and flavorful. Eat them, too, if you wish. But please, crunch in a quiet manner. And eat slowly, as always, savoring the tastes and textures, avoiding any unfortunate displays of grease or bits of meat on the lips and chin."

Then, as she chewed the heavenly little things with her mouth closed and tried not to listen to her stomach rumbling, he told her that there would be more shopping. And she would get better at it.

She didn't tell him he was frickin' crazy, but she thought it.

After the meal, there were more lessons. In polite conversation. In how to sit in a chair properly, for cripes' sake.

By the time she finally had her bedtime snack—an

actual glass of milk and one slice of lightly buttered toast—she only longed to escape to her own room.

Alone, she took a shower and brushed her teeth, greased up her hands and feet and put on the booties and the gloves. She climbed into bed and started to reach for the Miss Manners book.

But then she just couldn't. It was bad enough listening to Jonathan all day. She didn't need more of the same in her nighttime reading.

She tossed the book to the nightstand.

It was a big book and it slid off and hit the plush bedroom carpet with a definite *smack*. She didn't even bother to get out of bed and pick it up. Instead she grabbed the TV remote and pointed it at the television—but no. Forget TV. Forget everything.

She threw the remote down to the carpet, too. And she gathered her knees up with her greased, white-gloved hands and she put her head down on them.

And for the first time in eleven years, since way back when that rotten jerk Zachary Gunn broke her heart and she swore off men forever, she burst into tears.

She was so miserable right then that she didn't even have enough pride left to stop being a baby and suck it up. Great, fat, sloppy tears poured down her face and she let them.

Her nose ran. She didn't care. She let it happen, only controlling the flood in the sense that she tried her damnedest not to make a single sound. She gulped back her sobs because apparently she did have some pride left after all.

And she didn't want Jonathan to know how frickin' stupid and awkward and foolish she felt. She could do a man's job in a man's world—and do it better than most guys. She'd reached the top of the food chain on

an offshore rig at an age when most men would have
been proud to simply be holding their own as roughnecks. But when it came to being a woman, well, that
was turning out to be a whole lot harder than it looked.

She cried and cried, really letting go, feeling very,
very sorry for herself, biting her lip to keep from snort-
ing and sniffling.

And then her cell rang.

She decided not to answer it. She kept on crying. In
three rings, the call went to voicemail and again she
was alone with her tears and her misery.

Then the room phone rang. She tried to wait it out,
but the minute it stopped ringing, it only started again.

And she knew that if she didn't pick it up, Jonathan
would be tapping on her door, asking her what was the
matter, hadn't she noticed her phone was ringing?

Oh, she could just hear him now. *When one's phone
rings, Samantha, it is customary to answer it.*

If she let it get to that, she would have to reply and
he would hear her clogged, teary voice and know that
he had gotten to her, big-time.

No way was she letting him know that. She'd held
her own against some burly, badass roughnecks in her
time. How could she let bird-boned, big-haired Jonathan get the better of her?

She grabbed the phone. *"What?"* she demanded in
a soggy, broken whisper.

"Sam?" It was Travis. "Sam, what's going on? You
didn't answer your cell. And I called the room twice."

"Yeah, I noticed." A sob got away from her, followed
by a watery hiccup.

"Sam, are you all right?"

She clutched the phone harder, feeling ridiculous and
needy and weak and hopeless and sad. "I'm, uh..." She

put her hand over the phone, swiped at her eyes and then groped for a tissue with her white-gloved hand.

"Sam, talk to me. Please. What's the matter with you?" He sounded so worried, so...scared even. For her.

He was worried for *her*.

That meant a lot.

And then he said, "Sam, I'm coming over there. I'm coming over there now."

"No!" The word escaped her trembling mouth on a sob. "You can't. Uh-uh." She ripped a tissue from the tasteful beige box on the nightstand. "You know you can't. You can't even see me. Not until my final test."

"Forget the test," he said and really seemed to mean it. "It doesn't matter. None of it matters if you've had enough. It's not a big deal. We can call the whole thing off right now."

Call the whole thing off. He wouldn't mind or be mad at her if they called the whole thing off.

She could, she realized. She could do that. Call an end to this torture, give it up. There was no law that said she had to stick it out.

She could give it up and head straight for her private hideaway in San Diego. Walk on the beach, soak up some rays.

And then sign up for a new job on a different rig, go back to the challenging and profitable life she had made for herself.

"What about—" another sob escaped her "—your mother?"

"I'll find some other way to get her off my back. Don't worry about that. Just say the word, Sam. And you're off the hook. I mean that. Sam? Did you hear me? Sam? Are you there?" Travis seemed really worried that she might have hung up on him.

But she hadn't. She was sniffling. And thinking…

And coming to realize how very much she wanted this, how seriously invested she was in seeing the whole thing through.

"Damn it, Sam. Say something."

And she did. "No, I don't want that. I don't want to give it up. I want to…get through this. I want to make good at it because it does matter. It matters a lot. And that's why you can't come over here. Because Jonathan wants it that way. And that's fine with me. I am doing exactly what Just frickin' Jonathan tells me to do."

"Uh. You are?"

"Yeah. I am—and don't you dare tell him I said the word *frickin'*. Got that?"

"Absolutely. I won't. Whatever you say. But—"

"I *can* do this. I *will* do this. I am sticking with this program and I am going to get some serious girly going or I will die trying." She blew her nose, good and hard. By then, well, it didn't seem to matter all that much that Travis would figure out she'd been crying.

"Sam."

She sniffed, shamelessly that time. And it felt kind of good, really. It was kind of a relief. To let go. To cry and not care that someone might know it. "What?"

"Are you…crying?" He asked the question in a kind of awed disbelief.

"So what if I am, huh?" She grabbed another tissue and scrubbed her soggy cheeks. "So what if I am?"

"But you *never* cry."

"Well, I'm crying now. Or I was." She ripped out yet more tissue. "But at this point, I've moved on to mopping up the mess."

"So, uh, what's happened?" He sounded totally flummoxed.

She tried to explain. "Nothing. Everything. This is even harder than I thought it would be."

"It is, huh?" His voice was gentle. Understanding. "Listen. I meant what I said. If you want to back out—"

"Uh-uh. No way. I'm not giving up. I'm going through with it, no matter what."

"If you're sure that's what you want…"

"I am sure, yes. So stop asking me." She settled back against the pillows, gave one last sniffle. "I guess I kind of expected to be bad at this. I just didn't expect to care so much."

"Who says you're bad at it?" He seemed honestly puzzled.

"*I* say. And I ought to know—oh, and Jonathan, too. He thinks I suck the big one. He looks at me in that pained, superior way of his…."

"Wait. Jonathan told you that you suck?"

"He didn't have to tell me. It's written all over his snooty, pointy little face. As far as he's concerned, I can't do anything right."

"But that's not what he said to me."

She snuggled back into the pillows. "Huh? Said to you when?"

"When he called me a few minutes ago to let me know how you were getting along. He said you were making great progress and he was really impressed with you, that he hadn't realized at the beginning how much potential you actually had."

Now she sat up straighter. "He didn't. You're lyin', trying to make me feel better."

"God's truth, Sam."

She gave a very unladylike snort—the kind of snort she wouldn't have thought twice about making just a few days before. "And you think it would kill him to say that to *me?*"

Travis snorted right back. "Come on, you know how you are. The madder you get, the harder you work. Maybe he's figured that out about you."

She fiddled with the phone cord, twisting it around her gloved index finger. "Well, then why are you telling me he said nice things about me? Maybe I'll get lazy now I know he's only pretending to look down on me."

"Not a chance. You haven't got a lazy bone in your body—and it was pretty clear to me you needed encouragement."

She pulled her finger free of the coil of cord, feeling better about everything, feeling ready to face tomorrow. Feeling she could even handle the awful, disgusting shopping that would happen the day after that. "You're a good man, Travis Bravo. Thanks."

"You need me, you call me."

She made a soft sound low in her throat. "I think I can make it now."

"I'm here. Just remember."

He said goodbye a few minutes later. She hung up the phone thinking that she was a lucky person to have a friend like Travis.

Turning off the light and pulling up the covers, she lay on her back in the dark with a smile on her face. Jonathan had said he was impressed with her. Travis had been there to talk her down when she needed it.

She knew now she could make it. In only a few days, she *would* be ready.

She would go with Travis to San Antonio and play his bride-to-be for his family. Yes, it was a big lie and she didn't believe in lies.

But no one was going to be hurt by the deception.

She was just giving Travis's mom an excuse to take a break from her never-ending matchmaking, giving Travis a break, too. For a while, anyway, he wouldn't have women thrown at him constantly when he wasn't interested in anything like that.

He'd loved Rachel Selkirk, loved her deeply and completely, the way only a good, true-hearted man can love his woman. And he didn't want to go there again, didn't want to take the chance of being hurt like that again. Just like Sam didn't want to be hurt.

Sam folded her hands on top of the covers and stared up at the dark ceiling above and thought about how, maybe, after she got through the week with the Bravos, after she found her new job, she just might consider maybe going on a date again. She might consider giving love and romance and all that stuff another chance.

The thing with Zach had been so long ago. Maybe it was time she let it go, got her girly on in more ways than just her clothes and learning to sip tea without slurping.

Hey, a woman needed love in her life.

And Sam Jaworski knew now that she was just like most other women. A little taller and a lot stronger maybe. With a different kind of job history than most women had.

But with the same hungers in her lonely heart.

She closed her eyes and drifted off to sleep.

And dreamed of Travis.

It was a hazy, indistinct sort of dream. When she woke up the next morning, she didn't remember much about it. Except that she and Travis were together.

And in the dream, she'd started to feel sad because she knew it was all a lie and it wasn't going to last.

Because the honest truth was, she never wanted it to end.

Chapter Four

She got through the next day without once wishing she could wring Jonathan's neck.

Even though he pushed her constantly to do better, to try harder, even though he remained as snooty and superior as ever, well, she was okay with that. If Travis hadn't told her what her coach really thought about her, she never would have guessed that Jonathan believed she was doing well.

But Travis *had* told her, and his telling her had boosted her confidence enough that she threw herself into her training with new enthusiasm. She worked even harder than before.

And that second shopping trip on Thursday?

It wasn't easy, but it was better. She discovered she was getting the hang of what to look for, getting an eye for spotting the finds in an endless sea of different fabrics, colors and styles.

They went back to the hotel that day with more shopping bags than the time before. Jonathan couldn't help smiling at how well she'd done.

And she laughed. "I know you're proud of me, Jonathan. I can see it on your face."

"Ahem. Well. Don't get too confident. We have a lot more to do."

She nodded. "I know. And I'm ready for whatever you can throw at me."

His eyelids drooped lazily over those sharp dark eyes, a look of pure satisfaction. "Perhaps you would enjoy a T-bone steak, rare, and a large baked potato this evening as a reward for work well done?"

She clapped her de-callused hands. "Oh, Jonathan. You have no idea."

"An hour in the gym first," he ordered gruffly.

She was only too pleased to pull on the clingy, sexy workout clothes they'd bought that day and head down to the hotel gym. She kicked butt on the treadmill and then pumped iron for all she was worth.

And at six-thirty that evening, she was treated to the most beautiful slab of beef she'd ever seen. She wanted to saw off a huge, juicy hunk and shove it in her mouth, to chew without worrying about keeping her lips together, to let the juice run down her chin.

But she didn't. She put her napkin in her lap and she picked up her fork and knife and took her time about it. She cut each small bite smoothly and neatly—no sawing. She chewed slowly and thoroughly. She even managed to make polite conversation while she ate.

Jonathan didn't once have to reprimand her.

And it was….kind of fun really. Kind of graceful and satisfying. Eating slowly with care wasn't half-bad after all.

The next day, Friday, they "worked" her wardrobe. Jonathan showed her how to mix and match the various pieces, to make several outfits out of a skirt, skinny pants, a sweater and various accessories.

They also "did" packing. He produced a gorgeous set of designer luggage and showed her how to pack for various types of excursions—from a weekend in the country to five days in Manhattan to a tropical getaway and an Alaskan cruise. She laughed at that. At the idea of Sam Jaworski packing up her designer duds and heading for the Big Apple or Jamaica or the land of the midnight sun. She also practiced packing for the week with the Bravo family.

That day, they went out for lunch and for dinner. It was important to use her new skills in the real world, Jonathan said.

And the next day, all of a sudden, it was Saturday. The last day of her training, the day of her final test.

Jonathan told her what the test would be: That night at seven, Travis would arrive to take her out for the evening.

She worked her butt off in the morning, reviewing with Jonathan. It was something of a test in itself, to prove how much she remembered of all that he'd taught her, how much she could apply with seeming effortlessness.

Over lunch at Quattro, the gorgeous Italian place in the hotel, Jonathan actually praised her outright. He said she was amazing him. He said that he was proud of her.

She went back upstairs floating on a cloud of success and good feelings.

Then came the afternoon in the spa.

It wasn't as bad as the first time. She didn't have to get another peel and she didn't need waxing.

Still, there was the endless sitting as she had the manicure and the pedicure, the hair color and cut. She worked with the makeup consultant for a couple of hours, learning what products she needed, learning how to apply them.

It all took too long and she would just as soon have been down in the gym bench-pressing triple her weight, working up a good, healthy sweat.

But when it was done, well, she looked in the mirror and saw her dream self staring back at her, as tall and strong as she'd ever been—and yet, so much more. Even her too-short hair looked terrific, with highlights and lowlights, the gamine-style cut bringing out her cheekbones, kind of showing off the nice oval shape of her face. And the makeup was perfect. It enhanced her best features and minimized her flaws.

She returned to the suite, where Jonathan called her amazing for the second time that day.

By then it was almost six. Time to put on the beautifully fitted knee-length stretch satin dress with its skinny straps and built-in bra. A big rhinestone cuff and four-inch Dolce & Gabbana black lace pumps completed the outfit. She grabbed her small satin bag and the cute velvet shrug to keep her shoulders warm outside in the cool November darkness.

And she was ready.

When she came out of her room, Jonathan actually applauded.

She laughed and spun in a circle. "Pretty good, huh?"

He got out his camera and took a whole bunch of pictures. Sam almost felt nostalgic. Was it only Monday that they'd started together? Had she come so far in such a very short time?

It appeared that she had.

The firm tap on the suite's door came at seven on the dot.

She went to answer.

The look on Travis's face when she opened the door…oh, it was priceless. He actually gaped.

And then he said, his voice barely a croak, "Sam? My God. Sam."

She laughed in delight. "Oh, Travis…" And she threw her arms around him. He stiffened at first—because she seemed so different, like a stranger?

She wasn't sure. She started to feel kind of awkward, that she had maybe scared him by jumping all over him.

But then he relaxed. His arms came around her. He hugged her good and tight and he whispered, "You are drop-dead gorgeous, you know that?" He pressed his cheek to hers. "And you smell so good…."

She could have stood there, holding him tight like that forever. She liked it, so much, the glorious feel of his big, hard body pressed against hers. In his arms right then she felt so…feminine. Not soft, exactly. She was too buff for that.

But smooth. Definitely. And curvy. And very much a woman in every single way.

Reluctantly, she stepped back from him. They stared at each other, both of them grinning.

And Jonathan said, "Come along, you two. We'll have a toast." He'd ordered champagne. It was waiting, on ice, in a silver bucket. The bellman had already popped the cork.

Travis filled a crystal flute for each of them and then offered the first toast. "To you, Sam. I knew you could do it. And you have. You're incredible. I always knew you were good-looking. I just didn't realize how beautiful you really are."

She basked in his admiration and approval, thinking that the week of torture and starvation and grueling hard work had been worth it.

And then Jonathan said, "Sam, I wish you all the success and continued admiration you so richly deserve. When you get back here to the suite from your night out with Travis, I will be gone."

She felt teary-eyed suddenly. "Oh, no. So soon?"

He nodded his big head of beautifully highlighted hair. "Because, darling, my work here is done. I hardly expected what a triumph you would make of our time together. But you, my love, have come so far, so fast. I swear to you, my head is spinning. I will leave you my numbers. Do call now and then and tell me how you're doing."

"Oh, Jonathan. Yes, I will. And thank you. Thank you so much."

He waved a hand. "The pleasure was all mine. Check my website in a few days."

She groaned. "That's right. The awful 'before' pictures."

"Ah, yes. But also the ones I took this evening. I think any woman would be proud to look as you do right now."

She hugged Jonathan before she and Travis left him. He seemed so tiny and fragile in her arms. She whispered more thank-yous. And she promised to call.

They had dinner at Restaurant Cinq in a gorgeous hotel and art gallery called La Colombe d'Or. The building itself had once been the mansion of an oil baron.

To start, there was Petrossian caviar with homemade blinis. Sam had never in her life had caviar before. She found she liked the salty, rich taste.

Then came the toasted goat cheese, roasted beet and mixed greens salad, the three-chili rubbed pork tenderloin with Granny Smith applesauce and roasted corn relish.

Sam remembered to eat slowly, to enjoy every bite.

And even better than the wonderful food and great service was the handsome, dark-haired guy in the beautiful charcoal wool jacket and checked silk shirt across the snowy white tablecloth from her.

He looked at her so…appreciatively. As though he couldn't get enough of the very sight of her.

Okay, yeah. She knew this thing between them was just for now, just for tonight and the next week with his family. She knew they were only pretending, that it wasn't, in the strictest sense, real.

But so what? She didn't care. She was set on loving every minute of it. It was a new beginning for her. The start of a different kind of life.

Which, come to think of it, made it mostly real, after all. Yes, she was only going to be his fiancée for a week. But the woman she was tonight, in the black camisole dress with the lacy high heels and the sparkly rhinestone cuff—she actually *was* that woman now. She had re-created herself in the past week, with Jonathan's help.

Her new self was no lie.

They talked easily, comfortably together, as always. As comfortably as they did when they'd meet for beers at some wood-paneled neighborhood sports bar right there in Houston.

But Restaurant Cinq was hardly a neighborhood bar.

And the way she felt right now, looking at him across the table, the glow of candlelight shining in his eyes?

Well, it wasn't the same as when they went out for a beer. Not the same at all.

They spoke of his family. Of his brothers and sisters, their wives and husbands and also their kids. About how much his dad had changed in the past couple of years.

"He used to be a real hardass, my father," Travis said.

She took a slow, thoughtful sip of her wine. "I remember. You always used to roll your eyes a lot when you talked about him. You said your grandfather, James, was a tough guy, real mean. That he drove all his other sons away. Only your dad refused to go. He stuck it out."

Travis nodded. "And inherited everything when Grandpa died. Because no one chases Davis Bravo away or denies him what's his by birthright." He leaned closer. "Your eyes..."

She blinked and then gave a nervous chuckle. "Uh, yeah. I have two."

"No, I'm serious, Sam. Your eyes are amazing." At his praise, she felt a warm glow all through her. And he wasn't finished. "The way they tip up at the corners— and the color. Just a gorgeous blue. So bright. Are you wearing contacts, is that it?"

"Nope. But I did get some help from the excellent cosmetician at the hotel." She sat back in her chair. "You know, I could really get used to all this flattery."

"Uh-uh." He frowned. "It's not flattery, it's..." He glanced away. He seemed almost embarrassed. "I'm having a little trouble getting used to the new you." And then he looked at her again and grinned. "But I'm dealing. I'm working with it. And the view from my side of the table is spectacular."

She sat forward, too. "Thank you. I mean that—and now back to your dad. You were saying he's changed...."

"Yeah. He's...more patient than he used to be. Not so overbearing. Not so sure he's got all the answers before anyone even asks the question. More willing to admit that he's not always right. He's mellowed, I guess you could say. And that makes him a lot easier to get along with."

"I think I'm going to like him."

"I think you will, too."

"And your mother?"

He shrugged. "Other than the relentless matchmaking, she's a great person. Always there for her kids. All nine of us. She was born a Randall, which is a big name in San Antonio, and she's involved in all the upscale social stuff. Charity work, the country club. But even with all that, she's pretty down-to-earth. Not a snob, not in any way."

"Good. Because I *have* been thinking, Travis."

Twin lines formed between his dark brows. "You sound way too serious." His fine mouth flattened out. "You're backing out of the whole thing, right?"

"No."

His expression relaxed. "Whew."

She set down her fork. "But I don't want to pretend I'm someone I'm not."

His dark eyes grew darker. "Did I ask you to be someone else?"

"No. No, you didn't. But I..." She put her hands to her cheeks—and was surprised all over again at how soft and smooth her skin felt. Not really like her cheeks and hands at all. "I just mean that beyond the basic lie we agreed on, beyond my pretending to be your fiancée, and also beyond the new clothes and the new look and everything Jonathan taught me about how to…behave in social situations—beyond all that, I still want to be the same Sam Jaworski I was before I walked into the Four Seasons Hotel last Monday morning."

"That works for me. It's not a problem."

"Let me finish." She put her hands in her lap, laced her fingers together. Because Jonathan had taught her not to rest her elbows on the table until she was done with the meal. "I want my own history," she said. "I want my crazy dad who loves me and raised me after my mom left us, my dad who's retired now, riding around the USA in his Winnebago Adventurer with his new girlfriend, Keisha, who just happens to be four years younger than I am. I want to be the girl who came from a run-down ranch in South Dakota, the one who's just spent five weeks straight on the *Deepwater Venture* and is planning to look for a new job on land now. I want to be the girl who's had you for a friend ever since she was a lonely, oversize eighteen-year-old hayseed."

"Sam." He reached across the table. And when Travis reached out, she couldn't help but respond. She gave him her hand.

Instantly, something deep inside her went all soft and mushy. He wrapped his fingers around hers and the feel of his skin touching hers was so perfect, so comfortable and yet thrilling at the same time, so absolutely right.

He said, "You were no hayseed."

She allowed herself a hint of a smile. "Oh, yeah, I was. And I'm proud of who I was—of who I really am. We don't need to go into all that's happened in the past week, into my big makeover. We can just tell them we've known each other for years and suddenly, since we've been working on the *Deepwater Venture* together, we realized that it had been…" She hesitated over the scary word. And then made herself say it. "...love all along."

"That sounds good to me."

"You proposed a couple of weeks ago, the day before you talked to your mom and agreed that you'd ask me to the ranch for Thanksgiving."

"Okay, that'll work." He rubbed his thumb across the back of her hand. Her skin seemed to heat beneath that simple brush of a touch. "Did I say something to make you think I wanted you to pretend to be someone else?"

"No, you didn't." It seemed dangerous, somehow, to sit here with him like this, their gazes locked together, holding hands across the table. Gently, she eased her fingers free of his. She picked up her wine again, sipped, set the glass down, each movement smooth and deliberate. Jonathan had said that a fine meal in good company should never be rushed. "I just wanted to be sure we understood each other, that we're on the same page about how it's going to be."

He hadn't moved since she pulled her hand from his. He was watching her, his gaze shadowed and yet so intent. "We're in agreement, Sam," he said at last. "You can stop worrying."

After dinner, they went upstairs to visit the Colombe d'Or art gallery. Sam knew zip about art and recognized none of the artists' names or the paintings on display. Still, it was fun to walk around the beautifully decorated rooms and admire the bright pictures, her hand tucked companionably in the crook of Travis's arm.

Outside, the parking attendant had Travis's Cadillac waiting. He held her door open for her, and she slipped into the plush embrace of the soft leather seat without a stumble in her four-inch heels, without letting her tight skirt ride higher than mid-thigh.

"Thank you," she said as the attendant closed the door. Travis pulled away from curb. She turned to him. "What next?"

He sent her a quick glance, and then turned his gaze to the street ahead. "Depends on what you're up for. We can go to a party. Or walk around downtown. Or go see a movie…"

"Whose party?"

"Oh, just the CFO of STOI." South Texas Oil Industries. It was the company Travis worked for. She knew he got invited to a lot of fancy parties, partly because he was well-liked by the people he worked for. And partly because he was one of the San Antonio Bravos. She was quiet, considering. After a moment or two, he sent her another glance. "Sam?" He said her name softly.

A shiver went through her, to hear him say her name so low and intimately—and also because she was actually considering choosing the party over the safer activities of a movie or a walk downtown. To hold her own among the management people, the white-collar types. That would be something. As a rule, oil workers and upper management lived in separate worlds. If they went to the party, it would be a true test of all that Jonathan had taught her.

"No pressure," Travis reminded her. "Wherever you want to go…" He eased the car to the curb again and parked, but left the engine running.

She frowned at him. "Why are we stopping?"

He reached across and captured her left hand. "Whatever you decide, I think you need to start getting used to this." And before she could ask him what he was talking about, he slid a gorgeous square diamond onto her ring finger. She blinked down at it, all bright and sparkly in the lights from the dashboard. "A perfect fit," he said, and his white teeth flashed with his smile.

The party was in River Oaks, one of Houston's most exclusive neighborhoods. And the CFO's house was like some English castle, all of stone, with tall, many-paned, brightly lit windows. A wide, curving drive led up to the entrance and every light and chandelier in the place was ablaze in the darkness.

An attendant opened her door for her. And Travis came around and took her hand, tucking it comfortably into the crook of his arm, just like in the art gallery at Colombe d'Or. She looked down at her smooth, beautifully manicured fingers wrapped around his strong forearm, resting on the fine wool of his jacket. The big square diamond twinkled at her and she had a sense of such complete unreality.

Like Cinderella in the fairy tale, entering the ballroom already on the arm of her prince, wearing the magic dress created with a wave of her fairy godmother's wand and a healthy dose of bibbity-bobbity-boo. A modern Cinderella, though, one whose fairy godmother wasn't a plump, sweet gray-haired lady, but a skinny guy with big hair and a whole bunch of attitude.

It was a beautiful evening. She met the CFO and his wife and a lot of other people who worked for Travis's company. A few of them even knew who she was, being something of a legend, a tool pusher who was not only young for the job, but a woman, as well.

They all accepted her, treated her as one of them. Evidently, if you knew how to handle yourself and could carry on a decent casual conversation——if you looked the part of a woman that Travis Bravo might marry——

well, no one asked questions. Why should they? Appearances, in the end, counted for a whole frickin' lot.

She smiled to herself as she thought the forbidden word.

Travis leaned close to her. "What are you smiling about?"

She turned and looked right at him. "I was just thinking that I'm having a terrific time."

Midnight came. She and Travis were in the walnut-paneled library, sipping champagne. The ornate clock on the mantel chimed the hour. Sam smiled again as the chimes rang out. Nothing happened. She didn't look down to see her little black dress turning into a pair of greasy coveralls. Her black lace shoes did not suddenly become muddy steel-toed boots. She wasn't Cinderella after all.

Uh-uh. Her transformation was going to be a permanent one.

It was two-thirty a.m. when they got back to the Four Seasons. Travis had his suitcases already packed and in the Cadillac. In the morning, they would be driving up to San Antonio straight from the hotel.

He grabbed his overnight bag from the trunk and passed the keys to the valet. They went up to the suite.

Travis had his card key out when they got to the door. He stuck it in the slot and pushed the door open.

Sam went in ahead of him. She eased the shrug from her shoulders, dropping it and her bag to a chair.

With Jonathan gone, the suite seemed strangely empty. She wandered through the sitting room and into the bedroom where he had stayed.

Travis followed her. He tossed his bag onto a chair. "Strange, huh? The covers on the bed turned back, chocolates on the pillow and not a sign that Jonathan was ever here."

She sat on the edge of the bed and braced her hands on the bedspread to either side of her. "I was just thinking the same thing." But then, wasn't that how it went with a fairy godmother? They were gone in a sparkle of fairy dust as soon as their work was done.

And speaking of sparkles...

She glanced down at her left hand. The engagement diamond glittered in the light from the bedside lamp.

Travis said, "You were incredible tonight."

She felt suddenly shy and couldn't quite bring herself to lift her head and meet his eyes. "You think I passed my test?"

"With flying colors—and remember when Steve took me aside, just before we left?"

"I remember." Steve Daily was the CFO of STOI and their host at the party.

"He asked me where I'd been hiding you."

"In plain sight." She looked up then and laughed. "Wearing coveralls, safety glasses and a hard hat, on the *Deepwater Venture*."

He held her gaze. All night, he'd been doing that. He would look at her and she would stare back at him and somehow, neither of them seemed to want to look away. "I think it's going to be a piece of cake, getting you that job you're hoping for."

"Oh, I hope so."

"As soon as the week in San Antonio is over, you'll need to polish up your résumé."

As soon as the week's over...

She didn't want to think about it being over. Why should she? It hadn't even started yet.

But then she reminded herself not to get carried away

with this fantasy of being Travis's true love. The love part wasn't real.

She had to remember that.

The possibility of a new life in a new job…that was the goal here.

"I'm flying to my place in San Diego afterward," she said. "I'll get to work the minute I get there, get that résumé all ready."

He kept on staring at her, his eyes so dark and soft. "Good. I'll be putting out the feelers. You might have to take a serious pay cut to start, maybe pick up a few online classes to get up to speed…."

Actually, she'd been thinking of going back to school. Maybe full-time, to get a degree. But a starter position and some online classes were an option, too. "You know I can do it. Whatever I need to do." She reached down, slid off one lace shoe and then the other. It felt good to be out of them. She wiggled her toes in the thick bedroom carpet.

He said, "Oh, yeah. I know you can."

"And I have a good chunk of money saved, plus what my dad put aside for me when he sold the ranch, so I'll be fine."

"I know you will." He held down his hand to her.

She took it without really stopping to think that touching him, right now, when it was just the two of them alone in the room where he would spend the night, well, maybe that wasn't such a smart idea. She'd been getting lost in way too many fantasies about him lately, getting so she thought of him as much more than her good old buddy Travis.

Much, much more.

His fingers touched hers.

Warmth spread through her from the point of contact.

He gave a gentle tug.

She rose and he reached out and wrapped his free arm around her.

It was like a dream, a magical dream that she wished she wouldn't have to wake up from. He held her gaze, his eyes so soft, full of admiration. And maybe something more, something hot and hopeful and deliciously dangerous.

And then he moved in that crucial fraction closer.

Excitement crackled through her as understanding dawned.

Travis was going to kiss her—and not just on the cheek or the forehead, the way he did now and then. Not some brotherly little peck, the usual friends-only kiss.

Uh-uh. She could see it in his eyes.

For the very first time, he was going to kiss her the way a man kisses a woman he desires.

Chapter Five

Travis knew he shouldn't kiss her. There was no reason to kiss her right now, no one to put on a show for. There was only the two of them.

Alone in his room.

It was a really bad idea to kiss her right now.

But he didn't give a damn if it was a bad idea. He *wanted* to kiss her. He burned for it.

The whole evening had been the strangest thing. An exercise in shifting realities.

Being out with Sam, who was like family to him. Sam, for whom he felt frank affection and definite protectiveness.

Sam, who was the same Sam he'd always known. And yet…not the same at all.

Suddenly she was not only big and strong and smart and capable, a loyal friend with a hell of a mouth on her.

Now she was…very much a woman. All woman. In-your-face, sexy-as-all-get-out woman. Six feet of knock-your-socks-off gorgeous. With those iridescent blue eyes of hers that tilted so temptingly at the corners, that body that was strong and broad-shouldered and muscular as ever, but sleek and smooth and dangerously exciting, too.

And the scent of her...

He nuzzled her velvety cheek, breathed her in. She didn't smell like a tool pusher anymore.

She smelled of exotic flowers, of a tropical night, of spice and sweetness.

He couldn't stop himself. He didn't want to stop himself.

He touched his lips to hers.

Her mouth trembled slightly, and then went so soft and willing. Instantly, he was aching to go further, to guide her down to the bed, to lower those skinny black straps on that curve-hugging, eye-popping little black dress. He wanted to kiss her all over. And then, after that, to roll her under him and bury himself in her hot, strong sweetness, until she wrapped those long, hard, smooth legs around him and cried out his name as she came.

No.

He wasn't going to do any such thing.

He'd already taken serious advantage of her when he talked her into posing as his bride-to-be. It was enough—too much. He had no right to try to get her in bed. That would be flat-out wrong. She deserved better than that.

He gently clasped her silky shoulders. She made a small, way-too-feminine sound of regret as he put her away from him.

Her eyes were full of light—and questions. She lifted

a smooth hand, touched her lips where he had kissed her and she whispered his name on a sigh. "Travis…"

He caressed her short, silky hair, brushed it fondly with the backs of his fingers, thinking how he wanted to take her mouth again.

Promising himself he would do no such thing.

He said, "It's late. We should get an early start tomorrow."

She lowered her fingers from her lips. "You're right." And then she bent and scooped up those lacy black shoes. "Good night."

He just stood there, staring, trying to deny how much he wanted to pull her close to him again.

A smile tugged at one corner of that beautiful mouth of hers and she whispered, "If you want me to go, you'll have to move out of the way."

He blinked as he realized he was blocking her path to the door. "Uh. Yeah. Right. Sorry." He stepped aside.

And then he couldn't resist turning to watch her leave. The black dress clung to every tight, perfect curve as she walked away from him, her hips swaying just enough to make him ache for what he was missing, those sexy black shoes of hers dangling from the fingers of her long, strong right hand.

How easy it would be to go after her, to grab her free hand, to haul her back to him, wrap his arms around her, kiss her again and again and again.

But he didn't.

Somehow, he kept his head.

She turned when she reached the doorway to the sitting room. "See you tomorrow." She quietly shut the door behind her.

He sank to the edge of the bed, wondering what he had gotten himself into.

Thinking he should call the whole thing off.

And knowing he would do no such thing.

In the morning, he was up at seven. He showered, dressed, packed up his overnight bag and was ready to go at seven-thirty. The drive to Bravo Ridge, outside San Antonio, would take more than three hours. He wanted to be on the way.

But he hesitated at the door to the sitting room, his hand on the doorknob, feeling edgy and way too aware of that brief, amazing kiss the night before. It annoyed the hell out of him, to be all nervous and unsure—about Sam, of all people.

Would she be up yet? Would he have to knock on the door to her room and tell her to get moving, they needed to head out?

And then how long would he have to wait for her to be dressed and ready? The Sam he'd always known could be ready for anything in five minutes flat. She didn't need all that time for deciding what to wear and fiddling with her hair and putting on makeup, the way most women did.

But because she wasn't exactly the Sam he'd always known anymore, he had no way to gauge how long it would take her to pull herself together so they could get on the road.

He pulled open the door.

And there she was, sitting on the sofa by the picture window, downtown Houston spread out behind her, all dressed and ready to go. And she looked terrific, in sexy skinny jeans and a soft, clingy blue-green sweater that showed off all those dangerous curves he'd somehow never realized she had until last night.

Her suitcases were waiting by the door.

She rose to her feet. "Morning." And there were two places set at the table in the corner. He could smell bacon. "I ordered breakfast. Hope that's okay."

"Uh. Great." He felt guilty, for doubting her, for assuming that because she was gorgeous now, she'd be lazing in bed. She might look so good she messed with his head, but inside, she was still Sam. He needed to remember that.

They sat down to eat. He looked at her across the table from him, so fresh and pretty in the morning light, and he thought about Rachel, for some unknown reason. Rachel, with her long black hair and deep brown eyes, sitting across from him in another hotel room, years and years ago. Rachel, drinking coffee, nibbling toast, the future—*their* future—bright and full of promise, spread out ahead of them.

They'd been so happy, he and Rachel. They'd had no clue that death was going to snatch her away from him. That she would be gone from him forever within a few short weeks of that beautiful getaway engagement trip to Mexico.

He couldn't take that kind of loss again. He needed to remember that.

Sam was looking at him sideways. "Something wrong?"

He shook his head. "Not a thing." He polished off his scrambled eggs.

A bellman appeared with a cart as they finished the meal. Sam had called for him to carry her bags down.

The car was waiting, out at the front entrance. Sam had asked for it, too. The bellman loaded their bags in. Travis tipped him and the valet.

They got in, buckled up and were on their way.

* * *

Travis didn't say much during the ride to San Antonio.

Sam took her cue from him. She stared out the window at the highway ahead of them and she thought about last night, about the magic of the evening they'd spent together.

About that one sweet, too-short kiss they had shared.

She'd gone back to her room and gone right to sleep. And in the morning, when she woke up, she'd lain there for a minute or two, wondering if that kiss had been a dream after all.

But she knew that it wasn't. Travis really had kissed her. And she truly believed he'd wanted to kiss her some more.

She wished that he had.

They stopped for a soda and a restroom break midway. She offered to drive.

He said no, he was doing fine.

They set off again. Once or twice, she tried to get some conversation going. She remarked on the weather. She asked him a couple of questions about his brothers.

Each time, he replied by using as few words as possible. Clearly, he didn't want to talk.

So, fine. She had an iPod and her trusty Miss Manners book, which reminded her of Jonathan and made her smile. She read and she listened to music.

When at last they neared San Antonio, Travis turned the Cadillac north toward the Hill Country on a road called Farm to Market. Sam started to feel a certain restlessness about then.

They couldn't be far from the family ranch now. Soon she would meet his mother and his father, his brother Luke, who ran the ranch. And Luke's wife, Mercy, and their two children. And any other of his sisters and brothers who had shown up for Sunday dinner.

It was a thing with the Bravos, Travis had told her: Sunday-afternoon dinner at the ranch. They didn't all show up every time, but they all had an open invitation. And because it was the Sunday before a very special Thanksgiving when Davis and Aleta would renew their vows, Sam had a feeling there might be a lot of Bravos there that day.

She put the book down, put her iPod away.

"How you holding up?" he asked.

When she turned to meet his eyes he was smiling. "A little nervous, I guess," she admitted.

"You look terrific and my family will love you."

It was exactly the right thing for him to say. She forgave him for being Mr. Strong and Surly through most of the ride. "Thanks. I needed that."

"There might be a lot of them," he warned.

"I was thinking that there probably would be."

"But the good news is they're great people. I think you'll enjoy yourself."

She nodded and turned her gaze back to the road.

But now, all of a sudden, he wanted to talk. "Sam."

She kept her eyes focused front. "Yeah?"

"About last night…"

Her throat felt tight. "Yeah?"

"I think it was a good thing that I kissed you." What was he getting at? She wasn't sure she wanted to know. He added, "I mean, we're supposed to be engaged, right?"

"Right." Out the windshield, the land was gently rolling now, dotted with limestone outcroppings. There were oak trees and cattle grazing in the dry winter grass of wide pastures. Cottony clouds dotted the sky.

He said, "It would be odd, to pretend to be engaged without even having kissed, don't you think?"

She did glance at him then. He was staring straight ahead. A muscle twitched in his jaw. And she almost smiled, feeling a certain fondness for him, and sympathy, too, as he tried to get her talking on a not-so-easy subject. At the same time, she felt a prickle of annoyance. He'd shut her out for most of the ride—and now, when they were almost there, he suddenly decided they just *had* to rehash last night.

"Odd?" She frowned and turned to watch the rolling land go by out her side window. "Yeah, I guess it would be, to be engaged without ever sharing a kiss. But we're not really engaged, so what does it matter?"

"Sam…" He waited until she met his eyes before he looked at the road ahead again. "My mom has got to believe we're for real, you know?"

She stared at his profile, at his nicely chiseled jaw and manly blade of a nose. "How could I forget? Didn't I just spend a week and a big ol' pile of your money whipping myself into shape so I can pull the wool over your poor, trusting mama's loving eyes?"

He gave her another quick glance—one that almost made her laugh. He kind of reminded her of Jimmy Betts after she reamed him a new one for almost knocking one of the rock docs off the rig with a length of pipe.

"You're pissed at me." His voice was flat.

She almost denied it, but come on. They might be about to tell a whopping lie to his mom and the rest of his family, but right now it was just the two of them. The least she could do was keep it honest between them. "Duh. Yeah. I'm a little ticked off at you. You've hardly said a word to me all morning. And now, all of a sudden, you want to go into detail about how great it is that you kissed me. Not because you *wanted* to kiss me, but because we're about to fake being engaged and we need all the practice we can get to make it look real."

Without warning, he swung the Caddy to the shoulder and braked to a squealing stop. The guy in the pickup behind them leaned on the horn as he swung past them and went on by.

Sam pressed her lips together and stared out the windshield as the pickup vanished around the next turn.

"Sam. Damn it, Sam." He said a few more choice words. And then he was quiet. And then finally, "Come on. I'm sorry, okay?" He did sound like he meant it.

And she felt sorry, too, but she still couldn't make herself look at him.

He turned off the engine, undid his seat belt and shifted in the seat, leaning across the leather console. She was way too aware of him, especially now that he'd moved closer. He rested his elbow on the back of her seat, his forearm against her headrest. And then she felt his touch at her temple, so lightly. And then gone. "What *is* this?" he asked, his voice low and teasing—and puzzled, too. "You and me fighting? We never fight."

She undid her own seat belt. He backed off an inch or two so she could slide the shoulder harness out of the way. And then she turned to him. He leaned close again. His handsome face was only inches from hers. She could smell his aftershave. She'd always liked his aftershave. It had a clean, fresh scent.

"We never kissed, either." She glanced down at those tempting lips of his—and then back up into his eyes. "Until last night. First time for everything, I guess."

He touched her hair, the same way he had done the night before, brushing the backs of his fingers against the short strands. And he spoke so softly, "I liked kissing you. I liked it a lot."

She held his eyes. "Don't say it."

He frowned. "What?"

"That you liked it *too much.*"

He chuckled then. "You know me way too well."

"Yeah, I do. So from now on, don't feed me any bull. I can see it coming a mile away."

"You *sure* you're still up for this?"

She gave him a patient look. "What did I tell you the other night when you called me at the Four Seasons and caught me bawling my eyes out?"

He grunted. "That you *were* sure and I should stop asking you if you wanted to back out."

She leaned into him sideways and nudged him with her shoulder. "So what about you? Is it possible that *you're* the one who wants to back out?"

"Hell, no."

"You're not feeling guilty for trying to pull a number on your mom?"

"Sure, I feel guilty, but I want her off my case for a while. If you're still on, we're going for it." He started to retreat back behind the wheel.

She just couldn't leave it at that. She caught his arm. "Maybe you should kiss me again, before we go. I mean, how many engaged people do you know who've kissed only once?"

He stiffened, but only for a second. And then he took up the challenge and leaned close once more. "I guess I deserved that." His lips were an inch from hers. She felt his warm breath across her mouth.

"You know you did," she whispered back, loving the shiver of excitement that stirred just under the surface of her skin.

His glance slanted down, toward her mouth. Her lips seemed to tingle in anticipation.

Yeah, okay. Maybe she was playing with a big ol' ball of fire. And that wasn't smart. But there was a certain feeling of power she had now, knowing that Travis found her attractive, knowing that he wanted to kiss her, even if he felt that he shouldn't.

There really were definite benefits to being all feminine and womanly. Benefits she'd never understood before. It felt *good* to be womanly, to look in a man's eyes and see that he wanted her.

She thought of Zach Gunn then, of her one measly attempt to find what other women had—a little romance in her life, for cryin' out loud. Had Zach ever even once looked at her the way Travis was looking at her now?

She couldn't remember.

And truthfully, at this point, she didn't even care.

Travis said her name then. "Sam..." So soft and gentle, and with something like wonderment, too.

She had to resist the longing to lean in that fraction more and make the kiss happen. Because she wanted *him* to do it. She wanted him to make that choice.

And finally, he did.

He closed the tiny distance between them and his mouth touched hers—gently, at first. Kind of soft and careful, a kiss with a question in it.

But then she sighed in delight.

And that must have been the answer he was waiting for.

Because he slanted his mouth the other way and reached to pull her even closer, easing his big hand around the back of her neck, sliding his fingers up into her hair.

The kiss deepened. It seemed to happen so naturally,

so simply. His lips pressed hers more firmly. And she let her mouth relax.

And then she felt his tongue—who knew *that* would feel so good? But it did. It felt amazing, rough and wet and tender, teasing at her lower lip, slipping inside....

More cars passed, close enough that the Cadillac rocked a bit. She hardly noticed. She did think, vaguely, that they should probably get going, that it wasn't safe to be parked on the narrow shoulder of the road, kissing.

And kissing some more.

He caressed the back of her neck with his warm, slightly rough hand. And her skin seemed to tingle all over, as if his touch somehow set off a chain of happy fireworks under her skin. As if her body recognized these sensations he brought to life in her.

Recognized them. And wanted more.

Another shiver of pleasure went through her. She let out a low, excited sound.

And he moved his hand to cradle her cheek. His tongue stroked hers. His finger grazed her earlobe. And then his thumb was there, too. He caught her earlobe, rubbed it gently. The small, circular strokes thrilled her. Combined with the way his tongue was moving, so wet and hot and intimate, claiming the secret inner flesh of her mouth...

It was dizzying. Disorienting. Like looking down from an enormous height—say from the top of the derrick on the *Deepwater Venture*—looking down and considering letting go, sailing off into the sky, soaring over the blue sea so far below, forgetting that you didn't have wings, that you couldn't fly and the fall would kill you.

And that was too much.

A small, frantic sound escaped her. She slid her hands up between them, pressed at his shoulders.

Instantly he released her.

She opened her eyes, blinked at him, felt the world come bouncing back into focus again.

"Had enough?" he asked gruffly. His lips were red from kissing her and his eyes…they were darker than ever. She saw the heat in them. And some confusion. And anger—that she had goaded him into the kiss? Probably.

But why the confusion?

She wanted to ask him, but somehow, right then, she didn't dare. He seemed…almost a stranger to her at that moment. A stranger, and way too male.

She knew her lips must be at least as red as his. And her heart was pounding harder than it should have been. That scary, disoriented feeling hadn't completely faded.

"Yeah," she admitted. "I've had enough." And then her pride kicked in. "For now."

He almost smiled. "You always were too honest for your own good."

A certain sadness came over her. Strange. Her emotions were all wonky. She'd gone from turned-on to scared to sad, all in the course of maybe sixty seconds.

Gentling her voice, she reminded him, "You're honest, too, Travis. At least most of the time. It's one of the things I like best about you."

"So, then." He retreated to his seat and snapped his seat belt back on. The key was still in the ignition. He gave it a turn. The Caddy's engine purred to life. "You ready to go and tell lies to my mother?"

She put on her own seat belt. "As ready as I'll ever be."

Chapter Six

Ten minutes after they left that spot on the side of the road, Travis turned the car onto a long private driveway fenced to either side. Horses grazed in the wide pastures beyond both fences.

The driveway curved and revealed a sweeping turnaround in front of an imposing white house with thick pillars marching proudly along the facade. Wide steps led up between two central pillars to a long veranda. The front yard had been beautifully landscaped. Sam could see gardens in the side yards and even caught a glimpse of more gardens in the back.

"Impressive," she said.

Travis sent her a look. "The house is modeled after the Governor's Mansion. My grandpa James believed in living large." He stopped the car near the front steps. A guy in jeans and a cowboy hat came jogging toward them along another driveway that led around to the side.

Travis rolled down his window. "Hey, Paco."

"Travis, good to see you again."

Travis pushed open his door and got out, leaving the engine running. He came around and pulled open Sam's door, offering her his hand. She took it, telling herself to ignore the thrill that quivered through her, just from laying her fingers in his.

As she got out, Paco slid behind the wheel.

Travis said, "Paco, this is Sam, my fiancée."

Paco leaned across the seat to tip his hat at her. She smiled at him and nodded. "Hi, Paco."

"I'll have your suitcases brought in," he said to Travis.

"'Preciate it." Travis shut Sam's door and Paco drove the car away.

They turned together for the stone steps that led up to the veranda.

Right then, the big carved front doors swung open. A slim, good-looking older woman in soft linen pants and a white sweater emerged. She had sleek auburn hair and wore a welcoming smile. Beside her was a tall, imposing man with thick silver hair. Even if Sam hadn't seen pictures of them, she would have known who they were: Travis's mom and dad, Aleta and Davis. Travis had his father's broad shoulders and proud bearing. And his mother's smile.

"Travis! You're here!" Aleta called, real joy in her voice. She rushed down the stairs, her husband keeping pace at her side. When she reached Sam and Travis, she grabbed her son in a hug. "Oh, I can't tell you— I'm so glad you've come to us. It's been way too long." And then, breathless, she let him go and turned to Sam. "Samantha?"

Sam liked her on sight. She might be rich, from a

big-time San Antonio family, but Aleta was no snob. There was something so honestly warm and welcoming about her. "Aleta, great to meet you at last."

Travis's mom grabbed both her hands and gazed up at her all misty-eyed. "Oh, I'm so happy to meet you." She pulled Sam close. They hugged. It was a little awkward, but not too bad. Travis's mom was maybe five-seven, tall enough that Sam didn't dwarf her like she did some women. When Aleta stepped back, she shook her head, laughing, "I promised myself I wasn't going to fall all over you."

Davis offered a hand to Sam. She took it. He set his other hand on top of hers, enclosing it. "Wonderful to meet you, Samantha." He had cool green eyes. Watchful eyes. But he seemed sincere enough in his greeting.

Sam smiled and nodded.

And finally, they went up the wide steps and in through the big doors.

There were more Bravos inside—a whole bunch of them, as Sam had pretty much expected. Travis made the introductions, which seemed to go on forever, there were so many of them to meet.

Eventually, though, everyone settled down. Some of them wandered away from the big front living room into other areas of the giant house. It was not yet noon, and dinner wouldn't be for a few hours yet.

Sam had just finished chatting with Luke's wife, Mercy, about the drive from Houston, and the beauty of the Hill Country when Aleta spoke from directly behind her. "Feeling overwhelmed by Bravos?"

Sam turned and smiled down at Travis's mom. "Maybe a little bit."

Aleta grabbed her hand. "Come on. Paco's carried

your things up to your room. I'll take you there. You can have a few minutes to settle in and catch your breath."

Sam looked around for Travis, but one of his brothers must have dragged him off to another room.

"This way," said Aleta, and pulled her toward the foyer and the wide curving staircase.

Sam followed. She was slightly on edge about being alone with Travis's mom for the first time, a tad worried she might mess up and put her foot in it somehow.

Then again, Aleta was only being thoughtful. And a break about now wouldn't be half bad. There really were a whole lot of Bravos. It was kind of stressful, trying to keep the names matched with the right faces. Time to rest and clear her mind before dinner would help a lot.

Aleta led her to the third door on the left along the wide second floor hallway. "Here we are." She gestured for Sam to go in ahead of her.

"It's lovely, thank you," Sam said, "lovely" being one of those general-purpose polite words she'd picked up from Jonathan. In this case, it was the right word. The room *was* lovely, painted a sunny yellow, with carved white wood trim and white curtains. The cherry furniture was old and beautiful and her suitcases were waiting at the foot of the four-poster bed, which had old-time acorn finials. There was even a bay window that gave a nice view of the side gardens and provided a small sitting area.

The door stood open on the room's private bath. Another door, also open, led to the next room over. That room had blue walls and the furniture was heavier and darker than the pieces in Sam's room.

Aleta hovered near the door to the hall. She gestured toward the blue room. "That's Travis's room, through there."

"Ah," said Sam, for lack of anything better.

"Not his room from childhood. We never lived here at the ranch when the children were growing up. We would come, the same as now, for weekends and holidays. The kids took whatever rooms were convenient at the time."

"Yes, I know. Travis said you lived in town when he was small."

"Davis and I still keep a suite here. But it's really Luke and Mercy's house these days." Aleta waved a slim hand in the direction of the open door to the blue room. "I wasn't sure. Separate rooms. A shared room. Travis was not…forthcoming."

"This is perfect. Really."

"Good, then." Aleta folded her hands together. "Excellent." Sam thought she would go, but then she sucked in a careful breath. "I wonder if we might talk a little, before I leave you to yourself…."

Alarm bells went off in Sam's head. "Uh. Well, sure."

"Wonderful." Aleta shut the door to the upstairs hall.

Sam reminded herself that she *liked* this woman. And that she and Travis had agreed she would just be herself. Her *new* self, yes, but still, she had no deep secrets that Aleta might trip her up with—plus, there was no reason Travis's mom should even *want* to trip her up. "Well, um. Have a seat." There were two small upholstered chairs in the window nook. Aleta took one. Sam sat in the other.

"Travis has mentioned you often, over the years…"

"Ah. Well, he's always been good to me, looked out for me, I guess you could say. Ever since I was a lonely kid living with my dad on our family ranch not far from Sioux Falls."

"He always spoke of you fondly."

"He's…a good guy."

Aleta smiled. "Yes, he is."

"He helped me get my first job. And we've always stayed friends. And then, on this most recent project, we ended up working closely together."

"I'm glad that you know each other well. It gives you a good foundation to build on."

"Yeah. I…think you're right about that."

"You said you were raised by your father?"

"I was, yes."

"And your mother?"

The old wound throbbed a little, a scar long-healed but still sensitive if you poked at it. "My mom left us when I was three. She didn't much care for ranch life."

Real sympathy shone in Aleta's clear blue eyes. "You've never seen her since?"

"I have, yes. I used to visit her, now and then, in Minneapolis, where she worked as a secretary. But that was in those first few years after she left. When I was nine, she married her boss. He isn't a bad guy, but he's kind of shy, I guess you could say. I never had much in common with him. They had two daughters eventually—twins. I didn't ever fit in there. It just got easier for everyone if I stayed at the ranch with my dad."

"Easier? But you're her *child*."

Sam could see where Travis got his tender, protective streak. "The truth is, we never got along, my mom and me. I made it more than clear that I didn't want to be with her, even for a visit. I was pretty young, but still, I knew how I felt even then. I took my dad's side when she left."

"And why wouldn't you take your father's side?" Aleta asked sharply. "I'm sure you felt abandoned. I'm sure you…" She cut herself off. Pressing her lips together, she lowered her head for a moment. When she spoke again, her voice was calm. "I apologize for jumping to conclusions."

Sam grinned. "Hey, jump away. I *did* feel abandoned. And I hated her for it."

Aleta frowned. "And do you still hate her?"

Sam shrugged. "Not so much anymore. I'm older. I can see her side of it, too, now. We…keep in touch. Maybe a phone call at Christmas or my birthday. But we're not close. I don't think we ever will be."

Aleta reached across the space between them to clasp Sam's hand. Her touch was light. And reassuring, too. "I'm glad that you don't hate your mom. Hatred doesn't do anyone any good—and I'm so pleased to see you and Travis together. I've been worried about him, and driving him crazy, I know. Trying to get him to start dating again. To find someone special."

"You've been matchmaking." Sam shook a finger. She hadn't expected to feel so instantly comfortable with Travis's mom. But she did—comfortable enough right off the bat to give her a hard time. She leaned closer to the older woman, lowered her voice to a confidential whisper. "Travis told me everything."

Aleta laughed and confessed, "I *have* been matchmaking. I admit it." She grew serious again. "You do know about Rachel—and Wanda?"

"Yeah, I know. My dad still owned the ranch and I was working on a land rig, coming home for weekends, when Travis and Rachel got engaged. Travis brought her to meet us. It was a Saturday. She stayed for dinner. I really liked her."

Aleta made a sad little sound in her throat. "She was a lovely girl. You know he met her through me? Wanda, too."

"Uh-huh." Sam had met Wanda once, too. And she'd liked her well enough. Not as much as Rachel, but she'd seemed like a nice person. At least at the time.

Aleta gazed out the window. "I thought it would kill him when Rachel died. I was sure he'd never try again. But he did. With Wanda. And then I felt so guilty, the way *that* turned out. I wanted to make up for steering him wrong."

"Aleta, not your fault."

Travis's mom straightened her shoulders, refolded her hands on her linen-covered knees. "You're right, of course. And as it turns out, my efforts to find him someone new weren't required because there was you."

They both heard the hall door open in the room next door. "Sam?" Travis appeared in the open doorway between the rooms and spotted them. He leaned against the doorframe. "Okay, what are you two up to?" He was teasing, but there was a note of real suspicion in the question.

His mother rose. "Talking about you, of course." She went to him, kissed his cheek and patted his arm. "I was just seeing that Samantha was comfortable in her room."

Sam stood up, too. "And I am. Very."

"So, then. I'll leave you two alone." Aleta crossed to the door and paused before she went out. "Dinner at two."

"We'll be there," Sam promised.

Aleta shut the door behind her.

Travis waited until they both heard her footsteps moving toward the stairs before he said, "Mercy told me she saw Mom dragging you up here."

"She didn't have to drag me. Really. I like her. A lot."

He came toward her, looking much too manly and handsome in jeans and a sweater the color of dark red wine. "She's a charmer, all right. People jump through hoops for her. She's got that sincerity thing going *and* she has all the right connections."

"I think she *is* sincere."

Travis shook his head. "You've fallen for her. Just like everyone does."

"Fallen?"

He moved a step closer, lowered his voice. "I mean she's charmed you. And you trust her." The light from the windows slanted in on them, bringing out glints of gold in his dark brown hair. "You'll end up telling her everything, wrecking my brilliant plan to get her to let me find my own damn girlfriends."

"I do trust her, but I promise I won't mess up the plan."

He was doing that thing again, holding her gaze. Not letting go. She felt the now-familiar shiver, warm and delicious, as it moved through her body. "Travis?"

"Hmm?"

"You're looking at me *that* way again."

"What way is that?"

"You know, like you're going to kiss me."

He lifted a hand, brushed the back of his fingers along the side of her neck. Such a simple touch, to feel so good. To make her burn. "Would that be so bad if I kissed you?"

"No, I don't think so. Not bad at all..." She sounded breathless. Because she was.

He stroked her temple, touched her hair. "This...with us?"

"Yeah?" Definitely. Breathless.

"I swear I had no clue. I never thought of you this way."

She didn't know what to say to that. She knew he'd never seen her as a woman—not really, not until last night. And it hadn't bothered her before. She'd accepted that they were friends and nothing more. Somehow, though, it did kind of bother her now. She ached for her old self, for the woman she'd always been, the one no one seemed to see. It hadn't been all that great being the invisible woman. But she had learned to live that way, become accustomed to it.

Twin lines formed between his brows. "Okay, that's a lie."

She frowned, too. "What's a lie?"

"I did think about maybe asking you out at first."

"You did?" She wasn't sure she believed him.

"Yeah, but your dad said he'd kill me if I laid a hand on you."

Sam swore under her breath. "I never knew—and he's more talk than action, you have to know that."

Travis shook his head. "He loves you. And he thought he was doing right by you. And I like your dad. I wanted him to like me. So I kept my hands off. And you and me, we became friends. I guess I got used to things being that way, to seeing you as a pal and not as a woman."

Her throat clutched. If she spoke, she knew her voice would break. So she simply gave him a soft smile and a slow nod.

"Sam…" The way he said her name told her everything. She read his intent.

And she read him right. He cradled her face. And he kissed her.

Their third kiss.

It was as good—no, better—than the two that had

come before it. They stood in the yellow room, sunlight pouring in on them, and they kissed.

Her mouth knew his now.

And welcomed it.

He gathered her close, so tenderly. He cradled her against him. She drank in the taste of his mouth, gloried in the hardness of his body pressing all along hers.

She knew him. She knew that what had happened with Rachel had damaged him, deep down. And then all the awfulness with Wanda had only made him more certain that love wasn't for him. He probably wouldn't be changing his mind about that.

Not even for her, not even though he trusted her and cared for her and treasured her as a friend.

If she let this go where it seemed to be going, if she took advantage of that doorway between their two rooms, she would have to go into it with her eyes wide open. She would have to accept that she was one Cinderella who would get to keep the glass slippers, but would most likely have to let her prince go.

And what about their friendship? Even she, with her limited experience in the male-female arena, knew that bringing sex into a friendship—even a really solid friendship—could blow it all to hell.

He lifted his mouth from hers, took her shoulders and spoke with tender gruffness. "I could stand here kissing you forever. Or at least, until dinnertime."

She put on a teasing grin. "You're so easy."

He touched her cheek. He seemed to really like that—touching her. Which was fine. She liked it, too. He said, "But we should go back downstairs."

"Right."

He took her hand. "Come on."

She leaned closer, breathed in the scent of his aftershave, and kissed him again, a quick kiss that time. "You go on. I'll be down in a few minutes. I want to unpack."

Travis went to the game room and played pool with his brother Jericho and Jericho's wife, Marnie. They seemed real happy together, Jericho and Marnie. They were easy and content with each other.

And yet, they had that spark between them, too. Travis had always kind of thought that Jericho would never settle down. He'd been the family rebel, the complete bad boy, and he always said he liked his women tall and curvy and gone in the morning.

Marnie was short and slim, with a certain toughness about her, not what Travis would have thought of as Jericho's type. But they'd been married within weeks of their first meeting. And it had turned out to be a great match.

Travis won the game with Marnie. And then Jericho won the second game. Donovan, who was married to Travis's sister Abilene, rolled up in his wheelchair to take on the winner. Donovan was good. But Jericho was better.

By the time Jericho won that game, it had been over an hour since Travis left Sam upstairs. He started to wonder. Had she come downstairs yet?

Was she okay? Nervous about being surrounded by his relatives? Hanging back in her room to get away from all of them?

But she hadn't seemed anxious about his family. She'd breezed through the endless introductions, so cool and easy. She really knew how to handle herself around a crowd now.

And then she'd gone upstairs and gotten cozy with his mother.

The new Sam was pretty much a revelation, all the way around.

He thought of her room upstairs, of the door that connected it with his, of how much he liked kissing her, how he'd like to share a whole lot more than just kisses with her.

Then he told himself not to think about that.

Thinking, after all, too often led to doing. He'd always looked after Sam. And having sex with her wouldn't be looking after her. There were about a thousand reasons they shouldn't go there. And then there was the heat between them—the heat that made all those reasons too damn easy to forget.

He glanced at his watch.

A half an hour until dinner. Where was she?

He turned for the door to the long hallway that led to the front of the house.

And there she was. She'd changed into a slim skirt and a different sweater.

Their eyes met. Wham. Like a big bolt of lightning, searing him where he stood.

He realized there was no way he would last the coming week without holding her naked in his arms.

Jericho said, "Hey, Sam. Want to play?"

She smiled at his brother. "Eight ball?"

"That's the game."

"Sure." She went to the table, expertly racked the balls and then chose her cue from the ones on the wall while Jericho broke.

Travis sat back down. Jericho sank four balls and missed the next shot. Sam took over. He watched her play as he'd done so many times in the years he'd known her.

She won that game and then took on Matt, second born and CFO of the family company, BravoCorp. Sam ran the table that game. Poor Matt didn't have a chance.

She was something, all right.

But it wasn't her skill at pool Travis was admiring.

Uh-uh. It was the way the sweater showed off her breasts and the skirt hugged her body. It was the flexing muscles in her calves when she bent to sink a shot.

Matt's wife, Corrine, challenged Sam next.

Travis's sister Abilene sat down next to him. She leaned close. "It's good to see you in love again after all these years." Abilene chuckled. "You can't take your eyes off her."

He wanted to tell his sister to mind her own business, but how smart would that be? She and the others were *supposed* to think he was in love with Sam, that he couldn't help staring at her. He answered as a man in love would answer. "She's the best thing that ever happened to me."

"And you've known her for years…"

"Yeah, funny how that happened. We've both been on the same job for several months now. Working closely together."

"Working together. I know how that can be." Abilene shifted her glance to her husband, who sat in his wheelchair on the far side of the pool table. Donovan seemed to sense his wife had glanced his way. He turned to meet her eyes. They shared a slow smile.

Travis felt some relief, to have his sister's knowing eyes on her husband, instead of on him. "How's that dream house you two are building coming along?"

"It's finished," Abilene said. "We moved in six months ago. I love it."

"Good."

She turned to him again. "And you are out of touch, my dear brother. You know that, right?"

"Guilty as charged."

"I'm hoping Samantha will make you come home more often. I'm planning to talk to her about that."

"You're as bad as Mom."

"Not quite. But give me a couple of decades, I will be."

"You're scaring me, Abilene."

"Just don't be a stranger."

Right then Kira, Matt and Corrine's older daughter, stuck her head in the door. "Grandma says it's time for dinner." Kira was—what?—nine now? She'd always had a bossy streak. Apparently, that hadn't changed. "Everyone has to come and sit down."

Corrine said, "Tell Grandma we'll be there soon, sweetie." She banked a shot and sank another solid.

"Mom. Now."

Corrine sent her daughter a quick smile and took another shot. Two more solids dropped into pockets.

Kira pulled a face. "Well, hurry up, please," she huffed, and marched off the way she had come.

Corrine laughed. "My daughter is destined to rule the world."

Matt winked at his wife. "It could happen. After all, she's as beautiful as her mother and almost as smart."

"You're a smooth talker, Matt Bravo." In quick succession, Corrine dropped the rest of the solids and then the eight ball.

Sam applauded. "Oh, you are *good*."

Corrine grinned. "I'll give you a rematch if you'll

come visit me at Armadillo Rose. That's the bar I own in San Antonio. We're closed tonight and Monday. But Tuesday would be good."

"We'll all come," said Marnie. "Make it Bravo family night."

"It's a date. I'll expect you." Corrine hung up her cue.

"What do you say, Travis?" Sam sent him a questioning glance.

"Sure," he said. "Sounds great."

Corrine added, "And Sam, another thing. Friday is Black Friday. And that means shopping. We meet up in town at 4:00 a.m. It's the first year we're all going together—all the women in the family. We want you to come, too."

Shopping—and at 4:00 a.m., no less. Travis had a feeling that wouldn't be Sam's idea of a good time.

But she put on a big smile anyway, and said, "I would love that."

When they went in to dinner, Travis held out Sam's chair for her, taking total advantage of the moment to bend close and breathe in the faint scent of that tempting perfume she wore. "Having a good time?"

She sent him a look that flirted and challenged. "A *great* time."

"I'm glad." He took his own seat, smoothed his linen napkin on his lap.

They'd had the salad and the girls from the kitchen were serving the prime rib when his dad started the toasts.

The first was to having the whole family together. Everyone raised their glasses. Even the two oldest kids, Kira and Ginny, picked up their glasses of milk and held them high. Four-year-old Ginny was his brother Gabe's stepdaughter.

"To our whole family." Kira echoed her grandfather.

"Our whole family, yeah!" Ginny chimed in.

Luke's son, Lucas, shouted, "Yeah!" and sucked on his sippy cup.

Travis was starting to feel a little sentimental, sitting there at the long table with its embroidered white cloth. He loved his big family, and he was happy for all of them, that each of his brothers and sisters had found someone they wanted to spend the rest of their lives with. That his parents had worked out their problems and still held the seats of honor at either end of the table, that they were still giving each other tender glances, so proud of their children, so pleased with their grandchildren.

The next toast was for Abilene and Donovan. Abilene was expecting their first child in May. Donovan caught his wife's hand as they all raised their glasses again.

And he brought it to his lips. "You changed my life," he said. "Thank you."

Abilene's eyes were definitely misty. "You're welcome."

"You're a complete sentimentalist." Donovan's voice was husky.

And she answered, grinning through her tears, "You bet I am. A big bowl of emotional mush…"

Everybody laughed, though Travis didn't think the rest of them got the joke any more than he did. It was clearly a private thing, between Abilene and her husband.

Travis watched them together, thinking how they had it all. Just like his other sister Zoe and his half sister, Elena. Zoe and her husband, Dax, had a happy toddler. And Elena and Rogan had a big, handsome baby boy.

And then there were his brothers. All six of them.

Each had found the woman for him and then been man enough to work through whatever crap got in the way of a good life with the right partner. They were brave men, his brothers. They'd fought to claim their happiness.

Travis realized he admired them.

Maybe he needed to take a lesson from them—and from his sisters. And his mom and his dad, too.

Maybe it was time to let the pain of losing Rachel go. To accept that he'd made a big mistake with Wanda. And move on. To stop turning away from the possibilities life offered for fear of what might happen if he dared to take another chance.

He turned to catch Sam's eye. She gave him a glowing smile that had his heart beating crazy-hard inside his chest.

And when he reached for her hand, she gave it. Willingly. Without a second's hesitation.

She amazed him. She could hold her own with the toughest roughneck around. And then, inside of a single week, with a little coaching from an expert, she'd turned out to be one hell of a gorgeous, tempting, sexy woman, as well. Every time he looked at her now, he didn't want to look away.

He wove his fingers with hers as his dad raised his glass again. "And now, to Samantha and Travis. Samantha, we are so glad to welcome you as part of the family. Travis, congratulations. My son, you are one very lucky man."

Chapter Seven

At a little after midnight, Sam stood at the bay window in the yellow bedroom. She could see the waxing moon, riding high in the dark sky above the softly rounded overlapping hills.

It had been a great day and an even better evening. Travis had stayed close to her after dinner. He'd been frankly affectionate, taking her hand in his, laying his arm casually and possessively across her shoulders when they all sat together in the living room for after-dinner coffee. And then later, in the game room, when the two of them played checkers, he took any slightest excuse to catch her eye, to share an intimate glance with her.

He also touched her knee under the table. And he brushed her leg with his. He acted like he couldn't keep his hands off her, like he didn't want to let her out of his sight.

She'd basked in his attention. And she didn't really

care if he was faking it for the sake of the family. She was having the best time of her life and she'd decided to just go with it. To love every minute and not worry about what would happen when the week was over. The end seemed a long way away. After all, it was just midnight, barely the beginning of the second day.

She heard the hallway door open in his room. Because she'd left the adjoining door standing wide in invitation, it took only a glance over her shoulder to see the light go on when he flicked the switch in there.

"Sam?"

"In here." She turned again to the window and the crescent moon swinging from a star out there in the night. The soft sound of his footsteps approaching thrilled her.

He came and stood behind her. And he did just what she'd hoped he might do. He stepped close and his big arms came around her. She settled back against his solid strength with a sigh. He nuzzled her hair. She tipped her head to the side, anticipating the touch of his mouth against her neck.

And then his lips were there, so soft and warm. "What are you doing, alone here in the dark?" His breath fanned her skin as he spoke.

"Watching the moon." She turned in his embrace, slid her hands up his hard chest. "Waiting for you."

He kissed her. There, at the window in the soft darkness, with only the muted light from the other room and the faint glow provided by the moon.

When he pulled back, his eyes shone in the dimness. "It's funny…"

Something had changed in him. She felt it, *knew* it. She touched his lower lip, so soft compared to the rest of him. "Tell me."

"I roped you into coming here, into pretending we're in love."

"Uh-uh, you didn't rope me into anything. I came because you offered me the way to make some changes in my life. And also because you're my friend and I'll do just about anything to back up a friend."

He framed her face in his two hands. "Even something pretty stupid?"

She gave a low chuckle. "Yeah. For a friend like you, I'll even do stupid."

He traced her brows with a touch that lingered. "I want you to know…"

"What?"

"I think I've been played by my own game."

"Played?"

"I think I…needed for this to be fake. At first. Otherwise, I couldn't make myself take the leap. Take the chance." He shook his head. "Am I making any damn sense at all?"

She held his gaze. "You are making perfect sense."

He brushed her cheek with his thumb. "So…if this, with us, turned into something real…" Her heart expanded inside her chest. And the darkened yellow room suddenly seemed a magic and wondrous place, filled with light. He asked, "Could you maybe be into it?"

She didn't play coy. Coy wasn't her style. "I could. Yeah. No maybe about it."

He sucked in a slow breath, said her name so softly. "Sam."

She commanded, "Kiss me again."

He didn't need to be told twice. He took her mouth, his tongue delving in. She kissed him back, stoking the fire. And she pressed her body against him, drinking in the groan it brought from deep in his throat, feeling the hard ridge beneath his fly, the proof that he really did want her. Her breasts tingled and down below she felt so soft and hot, a melting kind of heat…

When that burning kiss ended, he said, "I don't want to push you…" His voice was low and rough.

She gave a husky laugh. "Oh, yeah, you do."

His mouth quirked up at one corner. "All right. I do." Then he grew serious. "I know you've been hurt, Sam."

She held his gaze. "We both have."

"And this is pretty sudden."

"Sudden? We've been friends for twelve years."

"You know what I mean." He looked at her so intently. As though he could see into her heart and liked what he saw.

She confessed, "Yeah, I do know." Joy. She felt such joy. It filled her like a golden light, bright as the sun. She laid her hands on his chest again. She could feel his heartbeat. And the diamond he'd given her caught a random ray of light from the other room and glittered in the darkness.

Somehow, the sight of that sparkling stone brought the doubts creeping in, turning the golden glow of her joy a little gray around the edges.

This magic between us started with a great, big lie….

And they were *still* lying to his family.

He must have seen the shadows in her eyes. "What? Tell me."

She touched the side of his face. "I was thinking that maybe we need to stop lying to your family."

He didn't hesitate. "Fine. We'll tell them in the morning."

She winced. "You're so brave. And all of a sudden, I'm a total coward."

"It's your call."

She wrinkled her nose at him. "You always say that."

His eyes shone. "Because it is—and you can look at this way...."

"I'm listening. Give me an excuse *not* to tell them. And make it a good one."

"All right. How about this? Tonight the lie is starting to become the truth."

She did like the sound of that. "Not bad." She turned in his embrace, taking his arms, wrapping them around her again, resting back against him, absolutely loving how easy it was becoming for her—to touch him. To *be* touched by him.

His lips brushed her hair. "I'm just saying we could wait awhile. See where this goes. Now it's not about my family anymore. It's about us. You and me."

"Us," she echoed, loving the sound of that simple little word. She gazed out at the moon. Really, he did have a point. They weren't lying to his family anymore—or they weren't *completely* lying. Not if they were really together now.

A lie is a lie, said a reproachful voice in the back of her mind.

Sam shut her eyes with a sigh.

Travis whispered in her ear, "Do me a favor."

She sighed again. "Anything. You know that."

"Don't overthink it. Decide tomorrow."

He was right. About everything. They would bust themselves to his family. Or they wouldn't.

It would work out between them—or it wouldn't.

That was the beauty of falling for Travis. She trusted him so completely. He wasn't Zachary Gunn. Travis was the right man to take a chance on.

This, for them, tonight, was the real beginning.

You didn't ask how it would end when you were only at the beginning.

You had to be willing. Truly willing. She saw that now. Willing to give yourself, willing to let the right man hold your heart in his hands.

Willing to open yourself.

Yeah, she might get hurt. Her heart could end up bruised and battered. But a heart, after all, was for loving.

And loving was about what you gave, not what you got back.

He took her shoulders, turned her to face him again. And he kissed her.

Everything made sense then, when his mouth touched hers. She put away her doubts and kissed him back. She drank in the taste of him, reveled in the feel of him.

A few moments later, he whispered in a prayerful voice, "I want to be with you, Sam. All night long."

"I want that, too." She touched his hair, at his temples, loving the warmth of the silky strands against her fingertips, loving that he saw her—*really* saw her—as a woman now.

"But I don't want to rush you," he said, so tenderly. "And I've got nothing. No condoms."

She gave him a slow smile. "We could probably manage to find some of those tomorrow…."

"Tomorrow." He made a low sound, almost a groan. "You're right. We need to wait." But his eyes said he didn't want to let her go. And he didn't let her go. He gathered her close again, kissed her some more.

Long, endless arousing kisses.

His hands caressed her back, moving lower, cupping

the twin curves of her bottom, bringing her tightly into him. So she could have no doubt of her effect on him.

Sam loved every touch, every brush of his lips against her own, every stroke of that hot, hungry tongue of his. She didn't want to stop any more than he did.

But she knew that they had to.

And so did he.

With a low, bleak-sounding moan, he took her by the arms and put her away from him. His dark eyes blazed down at her. "Good night. I mean that." He released her and stepped back. And then he turned sharply on his heel and started for the open door to his room.

Sam realized then, as he walked away from her, that she couldn't do it—she couldn't let him go.

In an instant, she'd kicked off her shoes, whipped her sweater over her head and reached behind her to unclasp her bra. "Travis." She dropped the bra to the floor.

He turned. Saw her standing there, naked from the waist up. His eyes flashed molten. He said something dark and intimate. She couldn't make out the word. But she took his meaning. "Sam, come on. Don't do this to me."

"You could…stay here with me tonight," she said softly, feeling suddenly shy and way too vulnerable. "We could…be together in every way but that one."

He said her name again, raggedly, "Sam…" It was a plea.

"Well, I mean…" It was hard to keep holding those burning eyes of his. But she did it, somehow. She didn't look away. "If that's all right with you. If that's…something you would feel comfortable with."

"Comfortable." He growled the word. And then he

came back to her in three long strides. "You have no clue what you do to me, do you?"

She felt a smile tremble across her lips. "Oh, I think I do. I think...you do the same thing to me."

He took her shoulders. "I can't believe this is happening."

"I know exactly what you mean."

"You are so beautiful. You always were. Why didn't I see it before? How could I have been so blind?"

"Stop talking, Travis. Stop talking and kiss me."

He obeyed. He kissed her, so deeply, as his hands strayed, skimming the tops of her shoulders—and downward. He cupped her breasts.

It felt wonderful. Perfect. Just right.

She started walking, guiding him backward, toward the waiting turned-back bed. They fell across it, kissing and kissing, pulling at each other's clothing, rolling, so she was on top. And then he was on top.

There were clothes flying everywhere. His shoes hit the bedside rug, one thud. And then another. His sweater landed on the lamp, his socks...

Who knew where his socks went?

They were gone. And so were his jeans.

And his silk boxers, too.

She rolled again, to gain the top position. And she loved the way he felt, pressed so close, skin to skin. At last.

He whispered her name as she kissed him.

She touched him, running her hungry hands over his broad, hard chest, tracing the sexy trail of hair that ran down the center of him, over his flat belly, and lower, all the way to where the hair grew thick between his lean hips. Then she encircled him.

He was so hard. She stroked him, still kissing him.

He groaned his pleasure into her open mouth. She had no shame with him, no shyness, even though she'd only known one other man, one single time, before him.

Her skirt was off and then so were the little panties that matched the hot-pink bra she'd dropped on the floor by the windows.

And then he touched her. In her most secret place. She opened for him.

And after that, well, she lost track of the world. Of time. Of everything.

There was only his caress, his magical, tender fingers making her body feel weightless and yet heavy and lazy at the same time. Making her rock her hips up to him, making her beg him not to stop.

Never, ever to stop.

There were no barriers. She felt utterly safe—and yet in danger, too. A tempting sort of danger, the kind that couldn't be denied.

He urged her onward, into the expanding hot light of her own pleasure, until she felt herself hitting the peak. Oh, it was wonderful. The waves of completion rippled outward, from her center to the top of her head, the tips of her fingers, down all the way to her toes.

Until there was nothing but his touch. And her body. And the slow, delicious fade into sweet satisfaction.

A little later, she took him to the same place he had taken her.

And then at last, side-by-side under the covers, cuddled up close, they whispered together.

They talked about their work on the *Deepwater Venture.*

She told him that yes, she was still sure that she wanted to try for a land job now. "This may sound crazy, but I'm thinking of going back to school. I mean, more than just a few classes. I have enough money put away to go for two years, straight through. With the online classes I've taken, I've almost got my bachelor's degree already. I'm thinking I might like to become an accountant."

He blinked. "That's a long way from being a tool pusher, Sam."

"I know, but that's okay. It's *good*. I'm pretty damn smart, you know?"

"I do know."

"And I want to try something completely different."

"You want to get out of the oil business?"

"Could be." She rolled to her stomach, braced up on her elbows. "But then, the oil business needs accountants, too, right?"

"Good point." He slipped a tender hand around her nape, pulled her close and kissed her.

When she lifted her mouth from his, she asked, "You think it's a bad idea?"

He brushed the side of his finger along the length of her arm. "I didn't say that. You just surprised me, that's all."

She took his lips again, a quick, hard kiss. "The more I think about the college thing, about *really* changing things up, the more I like it."

"I see." Then he asked, "Will you spend Christmas with your dad?"

With a happy sigh, she turned on her side, settling her head on the strong bulge of his shoulder, resting her hand lightly over his heart. It was a revelation, just to lie like this, together. Naked and warm under the covers.

He nuzzled her hair. "I asked you a question."

"Who knows?" She turned her head into his body, pressed her lips to the curve where his shoulder met his broad torso. Then she snuggled back down again. "My dad likes to keep all his options open the past few years, since he sold the ranch. He and Keisha lead a footloose kind of life."

He traced a heart at her temple—at least it felt like a heart. "Maybe we could come here, spend Christmas at Bravo Ridge."

She kidded, "Next you'll be asking me what I'm doing New Year's."

"You know, I just might." He brushed her hair back from her forehead. "Ted and Keisha can come, too."

"Right. Park the Winnebago out in front. So classy. Your mom and dad will love that."

He traced the outer curve of her ear. She loved the way he touched her, so casually—and yet so intimately. He said, "It's a big ranch. Plenty of room for a Winnebago."

It seemed to her he was pushing kind of hard on the Christmas thing. She teased, "I thought you said you didn't want to rush me…."

He caught her chin with a gentle hand and held her gaze. "I lied."

She scolded, "You know, you've been doing way too much of that lately."

"You're right. I'll have to watch it." He smiled. And then he kissed her.

After that, they didn't need words. They let their bodies do the talking. It was a very satisfying "conversation," even if they did have to stop short of letting go completely.

And it wasn't until much later, as he slept in her arms, that she started thinking again—or maybe over-thinking. Whatever you called it, well, she couldn't help but reconsider the issue she'd blown off when he first brought it up.

He'd said he didn't want to rush her.

And then, well, he did kind of seem to be doing just that—no, not with the lovemaking. She had made the choice on that. And she wasn't sorry. Not in the least. She was thirty years old. About time she spent a beautiful night with her own personal Prince Charming.

But really, he *had* done a head-spinning about-face that night. In the space of a few hours, he'd changed from a guy who wanted nothing to do with love—to someone who looked at her as though he couldn't wait to spend the rest of his life at her side. A guy who wanted to invite her dad and his twenty-six-year-old girlfriend to the family ranch for Christmas.

True, the change was a dream come true for her.

Still, something about it didn't seem right.

Sam scowled into the darkness. Then again, maybe *she* was the one with the problem. He offered her exactly what she'd been longing for….

And she ended up wide awake in the middle of the night, holding him close to her—and worrying that there must be something wrong with him.

Chapter Eight

In the morning, Sam's worrisome doubts disappeared.

Maybe it was waking up to find the thin almost-winter sun peeking through the drawn curtains—and Travis smiling at her.

She pretended to grumble. "What are you grinning about?"

He lifted up on an elbow, the gorgeous muscles in his arms and chest flexing as he moved. "I had a great time last night." His hair looked slightly blenderized and his eyes were low and lazy.

"Me, too." She thought about the things they'd done last night. Then she thought how they would probably do those things again tonight—and more, if they managed to get their hands on a box of condoms. Such thoughts made a fluttery weakness down in the center of her, made her want to pull him close to her, keep him there, in her bed, all day long and into the night again.

"You should see your face," he said. "Your eyes are making promises. And your mouth is driving me wild." He bent close—and bit her chin. It was a tender bite, more of a gentle scrape of his teeth against her skin, really. It didn't hurt.

But it did make that weakness in her center turn liquid. "Oh, Travis…"

"I love it when you say my name that way—like I make you weak in the knees."

"You do," she whispered. "In the knees. Everywhere…"

He eased a hand beneath the covers. His rough, tender fingers danced across her skin.

She moaned and let her eyes drift shut.

Several minutes passed before she opened them again. By then, she was breathless and limp. And very much satisfied.

It seemed only fair to make sure he was satisfied, too.

Somehow, they were still in bed at five of nine. She insisted that they shower separately. It was the only way to guarantee that they wouldn't get distracted and end up staying in their rooms for half the day.

She was dressed and finishing her light makeup, brushing on the final touch of mascara, when she saw him in the mirror, standing in the bathroom doorway. He looked so good, freshly shaved and wearing khakis and a dark blue sweater with the sleeves pushed halfway up his corded forearms.

He watched her with a definite gleam in his eyes. "Seeing you with your clothes on just makes me want to take them off you again."

She paused with the mascara wand a few inches from

her face. "Forget that. Your family will think we're a couple of sex fiends."

"So what? Happily engaged couples tend to be sex-obsessed."

"But we're not engaged. Not really." She went back to stroking on the mascara.

"But are we sex-obsessed?"

She decided not to answer that one.

He arched an eyebrow. "So, have you decided to tell them all that you're not my fiancée after all?"

She stuck the wand in the base, screwed it shut. "I met them only yesterday." She blew out a breath through puffed cheeks and admitted, "I just don't want to do that at this point. I can't believe I'm such a frickin' coward."

He made a chiding sound with that clever tongue of his. "Did you just say frickin'?"

She canted her chin high. "Hey, I may know how to dress and put on makeup and use the right fork now, but underneath, I'm as crude and unrefined as I ever was."

"And I'm really happy about that." He seemed to mean it.

And it mattered to her that he hadn't forgotten the Sam he'd always known. Still, she warned, "Well, just remember, I can take you down if you get out of line."

He grunted. "Doubt it."

She dropped the mascara back in her makeup bag. "Want to try me?"

In the mirror, his eyes flashed with sudden, wonderful heat. "Tonight. In bed."

"Bawkbawkbawk."

He came away from the door. In the mirror, she watched him approach. Was it just her, or was it suddenly hotter in there? His gentle hands clasped her shoulders. She shut her eyes, drew in a slow, steadying breath. He asked, "Who're you calling chicken, huh?" It was a threat. A really tempting one.

"Chicken?" She put on a puzzled frown. "Did I say that?"

He bent, kissed her neck, drawing on the skin a little. Not enough to leave a mark, but enough to send a shiver running under her skin. He caught her eyes again in the mirror. "Take it back?"

She turned to face him. "I guess, for now, I'll have to, won't I?"

He grinned. Slowly. "You will if you plan to make an appearance downstairs anytime soon."

As far as Travis was concerned, they could have stayed upstairs in their rooms all week. He could have called a pharmacy and had the condoms they needed delivered. He could have asked to have their meals left at the door.

Him and Sam. Who knew?

It was a question he'd been asking a lot lately—ever since he'd seen this new, exciting side of her. She was a revelation.

In the past six or seven years, he'd slowly come to realize that she was probably the best friend he had. His best friend. And now this. Every hour he was with her, he was happier with himself and the world.

He wanted to keep her safe. And at his side. If he could do both of those things, well, he'd be one lucky guy. The higher-ups at STOI were constantly offering him opportunities to work full-time on shore. He could step up to rig superintendent, with a number of company men on different rigs reporting to him. In fact, a promotion was available to him in the next couple of months if he wanted it.

So he could come home most nights. And she was making a change, too, giving up work on offshore rigs. He was glad about that. The work was too dangerous.

Accounting. Now, there was a job where you couldn't get hurt. He approved of that for her.

Well, except that getting her degree would mean she'd be putting in long hours in class and studying. And didn't accountants work sixty-to-seventy-hour weeks?

All that time. Away from him...

Anything might happen to her. The most innocent activities—something so simple as walking across the street—could spell disaster. He knew that too well.

They would have to talk about it, about what was the best choice for her, for *them*.

He took her hand, kissed the back of it. "You just *have* to go downstairs, huh?"

She eased her fingers from his hold and looked at him sternly. But her beautiful eyes were shining. "You recently spent a big pile of money improving my manners, and now you want me to be rude?"

He tried to look pitiful. "It's rude to stay here with me?"

"It's rude to go visit people and then not spend any time with them—which I don't need to tell you because you have a mama who loves you and brought you up right."

He had to admit he agreed with her. So they went downstairs.

When they entered the big, farm-style kitchen, his mom and dad were the only ones there. The older couple sat at the table, sipping coffee.

His dad said slyly, "We were wondering if you two would ever get up."

"Don't listen to Davis," his mom instructed. "You two are on vacation. Stay in bed every day till noon if it suits you."

Travis bent over her and kissed her cheek. "Thanks, Mom. We just might."

She reached back and patted the side of his face. "It does my heart good to see you so happy, honey."

"I am," he said. Sam was watching them. He met her eyes. Zap. Just sharing a look with her got him hot.

Davis got up. "How about my famous sourdough pancakes, maybe some bacon and scrambled eggs?"

Sam said, "Davis, I think you read my mind."

"Where is everybody?" Travis went to the counter to get the coffeepot and a couple of mugs for him and Sam.

Davis was already at the stove. "Elena and Rogan went out to the stables with Mercy and Luke." Bravo Ridge was a working horse ranch. Luke bred quarter horses, both for work and for show. "They took the kids." The kids, Travis assumed, would be Elena and Rogan's baby, Michael, and also Mercy and Luke's two, Lucas and little Serena. The rest of his brothers and sisters and their families had gone on home because they all lived nearby. Elena and Rogan, though, made their home in the Dallas area, and had driven down to the ranch for the week.

Some of the Bravo family relationships were…interesting, to say the least.

Elena and Mercy were very close. Mainly because Elena was not only his dad's illegitimate daughter, but she was also Mercy's sister, though not by blood. Mercy had been adopted at the age of twelve by Elena's mom, Luz, and Luz's husband, Javier.

In fact, until just a few years ago, everyone except

Luz had believed that Javier Cabrera was Elena's natural father. When the truth came out, there had been big trouble in both families. That was when Travis's dad and mom had separated. Luz and Javier had lived apart, too.

But everyone seemed to have worked through the old garbage now. They all got along.

"We're all invited to Abilene and Donovan's for dinner tonight," said his mom.

Sam grinned. "I'll get to see their new Hill Country dream house."

His mom, always big on touching, reached over and patted Sam's hand. "Yes, you will. It's a beautiful place not far from Fredericksburg."

Travis set Sam's coffee in front of her. She sent him a smoldering glance. "Thanks." He considered plunking his mug and the coffeepot down on the table, grabbing her, tossing her over his shoulder and heading for the stairs.

But then he had another idea. He put his own mug down in the place beside hers. "Abilene and Donovan's isn't all that far from the cabin…."

His dad had turned the burners on under the cast-iron griddle. He cracked an egg into a striped bowl. "That's right." He asked Sam, "Travis tell you about the cabin?"

"He did, yeah." Her gaze and Travis's met again. She wore a fond, knowing smile. It was good, he was thinking, to be with a woman who knew his history, who had heard all his stories of growing up a Bravo. She not only understood him better because of all that she knew about him, but she also had a common ground with his mom and dad and the rest of the family. She turned to Davis again. "He's always said it was beautiful there, that your whole family used to go there camping when he was growing up. Sounded like heaven to me."

His dad cracked another egg and agreed, "It's a beautiful spot." He picked up a wire whisk and started beating the eggs with it. "The cabin was pretty much a shack in the old days, when we all used to camp there. A few years back, we had it renovated. Now it's not only picturesque, but it has all of the comforts of home."

At his mother's nod, Travis refilled her coffee. He carried the pot back to the counter and suggested casually, "Maybe I'll take Sam to the cabin today, show her around."

Sam glanced at him sharply. And then she rolled her eyes—but quickly, so neither his mom nor his dad would catch her doing it. She'd guessed what he was up to. Which was maybe the drawback of being with someone who knew him so well.

So what? A few slow, deep kisses and she'd be glad he'd carried her off to the family cabin.

They could get condoms in Fredericksburg. And the cabin was cozy and private, with a nice, big comfortable bed in the bedroom.

His mom beamed. "What a lovely idea."

After breakfast, they toured the stables. Sam was raised on a ranch. She'd been riding since she was barely able to walk. She was brimming with praise for Luke's horses and the first-class operation he ran.

Luke asked if they wanted to ride, to get out and see more of Bravo Ridge. Sam said she'd love that. Travis started to get his hopes up. He could just picture it— the two of them, riding out alone, finding some private place in a stand of trees to hobble the horses and share a few kisses.

He was thinking they could spread a saddle blanket on the ground. Yeah, there was a nip in the air, but they could warm each other up real fast.

His big plans quickly crashed and burned. Elena and Rogan decided to go with them. Mercy said she'd watch the kids.

So it was the four of them.

It turned out to be a good time. Elena and Sam seemed to hit it off, which wasn't all that surprising. Sam got along with everyone in his family. For Travis, it was an opportunity to get to know his half sister and her husband a little better. Rogan and Elena had met a year and a half ago, when Rogan came to San Antonio to buy out Javier Cabrera's construction business.

Rogan was a big, good-looking guy with a winning smile, of Irish descent. Travis found he approved of the way that Rogan looked at Elena, a world of love and admiration in his green eyes.

They were back at the ranch by one. Mercy had lunch ready. So they didn't get away until two. They were expected at Abilene's by six.

That gave them four hours to themselves. Travis planned that they'd spend the majority of it naked in the cabin, rolling around on that nice, big bed.

But they had to stop in Fredericksburg to get the condoms. He pulled in at the Walgreens off Main and told Sam he'd be right back.

She made one of those snorty noises she used to make all the time, before the big makeover and her transformation into the sexiest woman on planet Earth. "Forget that. It's not like I'm some sweet little Texas rose. I'm not the least embarrassed to be seen buying my own contraception."

He gave her a long-suffering look. "I was more thinking of making it quick. You know, so we can be alone?"

"It won't take any longer if I come in."

"Sam, I'll only be a minute."

"You mean *we'll* only be a minute because I'm coming in."

There'd never been any arguing with Sam once she made up her mind about something. She'd already leaned on her door and swung her long, strong legs out.

They went in together.

And then, once she got to the condom display, well of course she insisted on acting just like a woman: She had to read every damn label. The only thing she was sure about was that he needed a large.

Which, he had to admit, was gratifying.

She was intrigued by the textured ones—for greater stimulation. And she kind of thought the ones with different fruity flavors would be fun. Did he want the "extra sensitive"? Would that give him a better experience?

A couple of other shoppers rolled their carts by while Sam rattled on about the various benefits and drawbacks of each and every option. Travis could have been embarrassed, but he wasn't. And the other shoppers seemed more amused by her candor than anything else.

And really, Sam was damn cute. He liked her frankness. And she'd always had a great sense of humor.

They bought six different kinds because she couldn't come to a clear decision about which of those six was going to be the best choice. Forty-five full minutes after he pulled into the parking lot, they were finally pulling out again.

The ride to the cabin was a pretty one, even in late November, with the rolling fields either mowed or dry. It was only a few miles from Fredericksburg.

They turned onto a dusty dirt road for the last half mile. And then, finally, the land opened up and there was the rustic old cabin in the middle of a wide, rolling field that in the spring and early summer was vivid green and thick with wildflowers.

Sam put her hand on his arm. "Stop the car."

"What the...?"

"Travis, come on. Stop. Now."

He put his foot on the brake and eased the Cadillac to the flattened grass at the narrow shoulder. "What?"

"Look. In front of the cabin. Somebody's already there."

He craned closer to the windshield. "What the...?" At the end of the porch, he saw two motorcycles parked side-by-side, shiny chrome gleaming in the winter sunlight.

Sam was grinning. "Looks like a pair of really nice choppers to me..."

Choppers. Custom motorcycles. His brother Jericho built choppers. And Jericho's wife, Marnie, worked with him at his motorcycle shop, San Antonio Choppers.

And hadn't Marnie and Jericho mentioned how much they loved riding their bikes in the Hill Country, and that they often visited the cabin?

Sam gave a low laugh. "Marnie and Jericho, that's my guess. What *do* you think they're doing in there?"

"Maybe we should go find out," he answered in a growl.

She chuckled. A maddening sound. "The blinds are drawn. I really get the feeling they're not going to appreciate being disturbed."

Travis couldn't believe it. Jericho had beaten him to the cabin. He grumbled, "We might have gotten here first if we hadn't had to spend an hour choosing condoms."

"It wasn't *quite* an hour," she teased. "And I really did have fun picking them out."

"Yeah." He slumped in the seat and scowled out the windshield. "I noticed."

She leaned across the console, hooked her cool, smooth hand around the back of his neck and dragged him closer to her. He was forced to meet those amazing, tip-tilted iridescent blue eyes. "Don't be bitter," she coaxed. "I personally hope they're having a terrific time in there." And then she kissed him.

And he forgot to be annoyed. How could he be aggravated when she kissed him like that? Like he was the only man in the whole world.

Like she could go on kissing him for hours and never get tired of it. He breathed in the scent of her perfume and kissed her back.

But eventually, with a reluctance to match his own, she did pull away. "Let's go back to Fredericksburg for a while, until it's time to go to Abilene's."

Fredericksburg. Great. The town had been founded by German settlers back in the mid-1800s. There were restaurants, a main street lined with shops and museums, a historic district, peach orchards and brew pubs.

He grumbled, "Now you want to go play tourist."

"Sure, why not?" She leaned close again. He got another heady whiff of her perfume. And she whispered in his ear. "Travis…"

"What?" He kissed her cheek. He couldn't stop himself.

"Don't be grumpy."

"I'm not."

"Yes, you are, which means you're lying again. And you said you were going to stop lying, remember?"

He turned his head so he could brush her lips once more with his. He couldn't get enough of the feel of that mouth of hers. "Lying *and* grumpy. That's pretty bad."

She was smiling at him. "That's right. You're no fun when you're grumpy."

"I'm disappointed, that's all."

"Yeah, and you're also a grown man, not some spoiled little boy."

"Am I getting lectured?"

"Yes, you are. I'm flattered and happy that you want to be with me, but it's just not happening right now. You might as well accept that. We can still enjoy ourselves, even if it doesn't involve the use of a single one of those condoms I spent all that time picking out."

He knew she was right. He'd been acting like a sulky kid. "Yes, ma'am."

"Don't make me hurt you. Say it like you mean it."

He returned her smile. "Yes, *ma'am*."

And then she reached down and put her hand on his knee. She used her strong fingers, massaging a little. He stifled a groan. She said, "Or you know what? We could stay right here. I've never used a condom in a car before…"

He knew that she hadn't. Before this, with them, she'd only been with one other guy. That SOB, Zach Gunn. And that was only one time.

He was seriously tempted. Enough so that his pants were getting way too tight.

But no. Just because she was so open and willing and sweet about everything didn't mean he had a right to sulk until she offered to do him in the car because the cabin was taken.

It was their first all-the-way time they were talking about. It should be in a bed. Not in his Caddy on the side of the road.

"Or," she whispered, her clever fingers trailing up the inside of his thigh, making him ache to haul her close, "we could get a room in Fredericksburg...."

He put his hand over hers. "Uh-uh." He gently peeled her fingers off his thigh and brought them to his lips.

Her eyes were soft as a summer sky. "Changed your mind, huh?"

"It's not going to kill me to wait until tonight."

"Coulda fooled me." She laughed.

He kissed the back of her hand, and then gently returned it to her lap. "So. Fredericksburg."

"Sounds like fun."

And it *was* fun.

They strolled along Main Street hand-in-hand, visiting half the shops there. At the Fredericksburg General Store, she bought a Betty Boop Christmas ornament and a souvenir billed hat that said "Happiness Is Drinking German Beer."

They stopped in at a bakery for coffee. He watched her gorgeous face across the two-seater corner table from him and thought how just being with her was the greatest. How he could really see himself spending his life with her.

And that kind of scared him. Enough that she noticed.

"Travis? You okay?"

"Fine." He picked up his coffee cup, took a slow sip. "Why?"

"You kind of slipped away there all of a sudden."

He had the craziest urge right then to take her hand—

the one with his ring already on it—and tell her he wanted to make it official. To make it real between them in every way. He wanted to marry her.

Right away, as soon as they could get a license.

Before...

What?

Before I lose her. The words echoed in his head.

But that made no sense.

Sam was just as into this thing between them as he was. There was no reason to think he was going to lose her.

And how could he lose her, anyway? She was Sam. His best friend. A guy didn't just suddenly lose his best friend.

Unless something happens to her. Like something happened to Rachel...

Rachel.

When the accident happened, the wedding was only a week away. The day before, Rachel's grandmother, in Dallas, had taken a fall. So her mom and dad had driven up there to make sure the old woman got the care she needed.

Because Rachel's parents couldn't be reached and he was the fiancé, he'd been called in to identify her.

Rachel, so pale and still on that cold steel table. Not Rachel anymore, not really.

Because Rachel was gone. Lost to him. Forever and ever. He couldn't get his mind around that.

Never to see her again. Never to hear her laugh.

Never to call her his wife.

He hadn't cried. There were no tears in him. There was nothing in him. A certain numbness. A will for revenge.

But there would be no revenge. The drunk bastard

who'd hit her was dead, too. He'd wrapped his sports car around a light pole a few minutes after he'd run her down.

Powerless. He'd felt powerless. Rachel was gone forever. He hadn't been there to save her and there was nothing he could do to make it right. His gut twisted.

And then he chucked his cookies. Right there in the morgue. He'd thrown up all over his own damn boots....

"Travis?" Sam's voice came to him. Her face swam into view.

What the hell did he think he was doing, anyway?

Wasn't it only yesterday morning that he'd sat across from Sam in the suite at the Four Seasons and told himself he would never leave himself open for that kind of pain again?

"Travis? Travis, are you okay?" Sam leaned toward him across the table. There was a world of worry in those blue eyes of hers.

He blinked, shook his head. "Fine. Really. Didn't I already say that?"

"You don't look so good." She reached out.

He caught her hand. Her capable, soft, strong hand.

And everything changed. Just from the touch of her hand.

All at once, he was...okay. Truly okay. His crazy, irrational fears receded.

There was just him. And Sam. In this cute little bakery. Sharing the afternoon before heading to his sister's for a family dinner.

"Sorry," he said. And he leaned across the table.

She still had questions in her eyes. But she met him halfway, shared the kiss he offered, a quick, innocent kiss, given that they were sitting in a public place. "But are you—?"

He didn't let her finish. "I mean it. It's nothing."

She freed her hand from his and sank back to her chair. "So how come I don't believe you?"

"Sam." He waited for her to meet his gaze. "I was just daydreaming, that's all."

"You didn't look like you were daydreaming." She kept her voice low, for his ears alone. "You looked like you saw a ghost."

A ghost. Well, in a way, he had. But he wasn't seeing a ghost now. He saw only Sam. Everything would be all right. He was ready for this. Ready at last. "No ghost. I promise you."

She opened her mouth to say something—and then she changed her mind. Instead, she picked up her coffee cup, sipped from it, set it carefully down. And then she turned her head to stare out the window.

He just sat there. He knew her so well. She wasn't the kind to push and prod at a man. All he had to do was wait.

It worked. After a minute, she turned to him again. "I would..." She seemed to fumble for the right words. "You know I'm here, right? Anything you say to me, I can take it."

"I know." He said it firmly but gently. "But there's nothing."

She glanced away again, but only for a second. Then she resolutely faced him once more. She sucked in a slow breath and she made herself smile. "Well, okay, then. If you say so."

Chapter Nine

Other than the strange and unsettling incident in the bakery, Sam had a great time that afternoon and evening. She and Travis toured the Pioneer Museum before heading for Abilene's house.

The house was southeast of Fredericksburg on a beautiful piece of land, with a clear creek running in the back and a view of craggy limestone peaks from the kitchen windows. It had a giant great room at its heart and an extra kitchen outside for use in the warmer months of the year. It was on two levels, with an elevator as well as a staircase, so that Donovan could get around with ease in his wheelchair.

By six-fifteen, everyone in the family was there—except for Jericho and Marnie. They rolled up on their choppers at six-thirty, looking windblown and slightly flushed and way too pleased with themselves.

The family was gathered in the great room then, filling the vaulted space with lively conversation and the occasional burst of shared laughter. They sipped cold drinks and munched finger-food appetizers. All the kids who were old enough to walk were either playing with Abilene's two rescue kittens or following her three mutt dogs around, trying to pet them.

Travis leaned close to Sam when Jericho and his wife came in. "They look happy."

She whispered back, "Well, who doesn't enjoy a nice, long...ride?"

He laughed and put an arm around her, drawing her close to brush a kiss at her temple. Aleta happened to be sitting in her line of sight. Travis's mom saw their interaction, including the quick, affectionate kiss. And she beamed in motherly satisfaction.

Sam realized she no longer felt guilty for pretending to be engaged. There really was nothing to feel that guilty about anymore. She and Travis were...what?

The word came to her: *serious.*

Yeah. They were serious about each other, about this longtime friendship of theirs that had bloomed overnight into something so much more. Something so sweet and real. And hot.

Sam was glad it pleased Aleta to see them together. His mom seemed to believe that all Travis had ever needed was to let go of the past and find a good woman to make his life complete.

Maybe that was true. Sam didn't mind at all thinking of herself as the good woman his mama had been hoping he'd find. The only thing that nagged at her was the question of whether he'd really let the past go—or if maybe there was something else that was eating at him. She needed to talk to him about that.

But somehow, so far, she hadn't found a way to *get* him to talk about it. Which was weird in itself.

She and Travis had always been able to talk about everything. He knew all her secrets.

And she was the one he came to when he needed to talk. She knew how much he'd suffered when he lost Rachel. And how rotten he'd felt when Wanda took off with another guy, how he'd blamed himself. Because he was still in love with Rachel—or at least, with the memory of Rachel. And Wanda had known.

But today, in the bakery, he'd lied right to her face. She'd seen the stricken look in his eyes. Yet he'd insisted that there was nothing wrong. She should probably have kept after him, not given up until he busted to the truth.

Then again, well, everything was changing between them now. They were creating a whole new kind of relationship. Maybe she needed to be patient with him, give him time to get used to being more than just friends, time to open up to her the way he always had before.

His warm fingers closed over hers. Everyone was going in to eat. Holding hands, side-by-side, they followed the crowd to the dining room.

Travis couldn't wait to get Sam back to their rooms at Bravo Ridge.

But they stayed at Abilene's until midnight after all. They played Texas Hold'em with Abilene, Donovan, Jericho and Marnie. It was fun, really. And he knew Sam was having a great time.

When he finally eased the Cadillac into the six-car garage down the curving path at the side of the ranch house, all was quiet. Luke and Mercy, Elena and Rogan, and their kids had returned earlier. So had his parents.

He and Sam went in the front door and tiptoed up the stairs together. The second he got her inside his room, he pushed the door shut and turned the privacy lock. He tipped up her chin and found her mouth in the darkness.

"Wait here," he whispered against her sweet, parted lips.

She made a low, questioning sound, but she didn't say anything.

He left her to turn on a lamp. And before he went to her again, he detoured through the open door to her room. He engaged the privacy lock on the hall door in there.

He was back at her side in seconds. "Alone at last," he whispered.

She laughed and shook the Walgreens bag she'd carried in from the car. "With plenty of condoms."

"All is right with the world." He took her free hand and pulled her over to the side of the turned-down bed.

And then he took her in his arms.

The Walgreens bag dropped to the rug as she kissed him. Within maybe sixty seconds, her clothes and his clothes were in a pile at their feet.

They had to stop kissing to dig through all the clothing and retrieve the bag.

"Got it." She held it up with a triumphant smile.

He grabbed her wrist, pulled her to her feet—and back into his arms. He couldn't get enough of the silky, strong feel of her body, of her full, firm breasts and her shapely wide shoulders. He stroked her back, tracing the bumps of her spine. And then he slipped a hand between them, drinking in her gasp of excitement as he dipped a finger into the wet heat of her.

She was so ready. And so was he.

He needed to be inside her, joined with her. But he tried to remember that there had been only one other time for her, all those years ago, and that that one time hadn't been good. He forced himself to take it slow, using his thumb to tease the swollen heart of her pleasure, dipping his fingers inside.

She moved against his touch, moaning, and he felt her inner muscles relaxing, felt the greater wetness. He eased another finger in. She sighed in pleasure. He knew she was right at the edge.

But she didn't allow him to take her over. Instead, she pushed him onto the bed and followed him down. The Walgreens bag crackled as it ended up under him. Her mouth still fused to his, she gave a tug and freed it.

And then she broke the scorching kiss. She was pulling away from him.

He tried to catch her, to take her lips again and resume the kiss, to regain the deep and intimate touch. But she was quicker.

Laughing and breathless, her face and upper chest flushed with excited color, she sat back against the pillows. Gathering her gorgeous, muscular legs up, crossing them yoga-style, she opened the bag. "Hmm, what do we have here?"

"You," he said darkly, still flat on his back, his desire for her way too evident. "You're driving me crazy. You know that, right?" With her legs crossed like that, he could see everything, all sweet and pink and so temptingly wet for him. And it wasn't only that. It was the sheer animal beauty of her, the strength and power in every sleek, smooth inch.

She reminded him of the women in the science fiction novels he couldn't get enough of as a kid—warrior women, tall and commanding, who lived in strange jungles on faraway planets, who dressed in leather pelts and hammered silver and hunted fantastical creatures using only a shield and spear. Women who didn't need men—or thought they didn't.

Until the right spaceship captain dropped out of the sky.

"I think…this one." She pulled a shiny red box from the bag and dropped the bag onto the nightstand.

As if he cared which one she chose. He grabbed her ankle. "Come back here."

"Patience, patience." She reached down, peeled his fingers free, brought them to her lips—and sucked his index finger into her mouth. He almost lost it right there. And then she rubbed her tongue around it. He gritted his teeth, closed his eyes and looked away. Finally, she let his finger go. And she teased, "A well isn't drilled in a day."

He groaned and turned to look at her again. It made him ache to look, but it was a glorious kind of pain. "Don't talk about drilling," he pleaded. "It just isn't fair."

"Whoever told you it was going to be fair?" She opened the box and removed a wrapped pouch. Then, taking her sweet, agonizing time about it, she shut the box and set it on the nightstand with the bag. "Hmm." She neatly tore the wrapper off the pouch.

And then, just like that, her bright, bold confidence vanished. Holding the naked-looking circle of lubricated latex, she bit her lip and sighed. He saw the shy and tender woman within, the one she'd spent years trying to hide from the tough, able men who worked in the oil business.

His heart turned to mush.

That time when he reached to touch her, it was to soothe her. He clasped her knee, lightly, gently. "Hey. Okay?"

She confessed, her head tipped down, "I'm a little… nervous, I guess."

He sat up then, scooted around beside her, and laid an arm across her velvety-smooth shoulders. Drawing her close to him, he guided her head down against his chest. "We don't have to do this right now."

She gave a sad little chuckle. "That's not what you've been saying all afternoon."

He smoothed her hair, rubbed her shoulder. "I'm sorry. I know I was an ass this afternoon."

Of course she had to jump to his defense. "No, you weren't."

"I was." He kissed the crown of her head, loving the clean, silky feel of her hair against his mouth, enjoying her fresh scent. "I do want you. So bad. It's like a revelation to me, you know? You and me. Together. After all these years."

"Yeah, I get that. I know what you mean. It's the same for me."

"But, Sam, I can wait until you're ready. Until you're…comfortable."

"I *am* comfortable. It's only…" She lifted her head and they gazed at each other. She admitted in a small voice, "It was pretty bad, that one time with Zach."

Zach Gunn. The bastard. He said intently, "The guy was a major jerk."

"I took the wrapper off this thing—" she still had the condom in her hand "—and it all came back. How rough he was. How much it hurt. How I tried to be…I don't know, brave. Tough. To act like I knew what I was doing. And it only got worse. It only hurt more. But I stuck it out. And then afterward, he went and told everyone how bad I was in bed. He said I might be female, but I sure wasn't a real woman. No wonder I was stronger than half the guys on the rig."

Listening to her now, seeing the old pain haunt her eyes, he wished he could get that SOB alone again, rearrange his face a second time. "You *are* a woman. *All* woman."

A wobbly smile came and went. "Oh, Travis..."

"And I would never do you that way. I couldn't stand to hurt you. And what happens between us, that's only between us."

"I know."

He gave her a coaxing smile. "Though if I *did* talk about you—which I never would—it would only be about how amazing and beautiful you are. How I can't get enough of you. How you drive me stark raving out of my mind and I sincerely hope you will continue to do so for a long, long time to come."

Hesitantly, she lifted her free hand. Her fingers brushed the side of his face, so lightly, before she withdrew them. "But the things that have happened to us in the past...they can be powerful. They can still have a grip on us. If we let them, they can destroy our happiness. They can ruin what we have now. You know?" Her eyes searched his.

And he realized she wasn't talking about only herself. She meant those bad moments he'd had in the bakery in the afternoon. "The past is not going to ruin what we have, Sam." He spoke slowly. Deliberately. "I won't let it. *We* won't let it."

She sucked in a trembling breath. "You sound so sure."

"Because I *am* sure."

"Well." She smiled again, a much brighter smile. "That's good. That's really good." She held up the condom. Gulped. And then her gaze dropped to his lap. She touched him—a shy touch, quickly withdrawn. "Looks like I kind of...ruined the mood."

But the brief caress was all it took. He felt the warm ache of arousal and began to grow hard again. "Not a problem," he told her gruffly. "I'm easy when it comes to you."

"Oh, yeah. I like that about you. I like it a lot." She reached out again and her cool, smooth fingers closed around him.

Now he was the one gulping. He stifled a moan.

She asked, "Is it all right if I...?"

He did moan then. "Anything. Everything..."

She stroked him, long slow strokes. And then she shifted her legs around, folding them under her. She lowered her mouth and she took him inside.

Her soft, slick wetness surrounded him. She drew on him, rhythmically.

He wove his fingers in her hair, guiding her a little, wishing he could last forever. But within a few too-brief minutes, he was way too close to letting go.

He took her shoulders. "I can't...no more..."

With a sigh, she sat back on her folded knees. Her lips were shiny and red. So kissable. And the flush was back on her high cheekbones.

He pulled her toward him again, covered her mouth with his own. They shared one of those kisses that lit up the night.

Finally, she whispered, her lips moving against his, "Is it okay if I...put it on you?"

"Yeah. It's okay. It's more than okay." He brushed

his mouth back and forth on hers as he spoke. He pulled away enough that they could share a smile.

Then they drew apart.

With care, she positioned the condom and rolled it down into place. "There." She sat back on her folded knees again and slanted him a look. "So…maybe if I kind of let you take over from here?"

"Whatever you want, Sam. I mean that."

"Okay." She stretched out beside him on her back and shut her eyes. "Go ahead, then." Her voice had a barely-discernable tremor.

For a moment, he just sat there, staring at her long, strong body, at her soft lips and closed eyes. He wanted to make it good for her. He wanted to wipe out the only memory she had of what might happen between a man and a woman.

He wanted to be the only man she thought of when she thought of this.

He made the first touch feather-light. With a finger, he traced her brows. A small sound escaped her—of anticipation or anxiety? He couldn't tell which.

"You're so beautiful, Sam…." He traced the bridge of her nose, the curve of her forehead, the tender indentation at each temple, the high crests of her cheekbones.

And then he bent close. He kissed the places he had already touched.

By the time he settled his lips onto hers, she was smiling a little. She opened to welcome him.

He drew that kiss out forever. It lasted even longer than some of the other endless kisses they had shared. With his lips and his tongue, he urged her to forget whatever fears she had, to be easy inside herself.

To let bad memories go.

As he kissed her, he touched her, slowly and thoroughly, the way he had the night before.

He cradled her breasts, teasing the nipples until she lifted toward him and moaned her excitement. Only then did he take the caress lower. He rubbed her flat belly. He ran his hands down the twin curves of her hips.

And he stroked her thighs.

In time, she began to move her hips, inviting him. She whispered breathless encouragements against his lips. "Yes. Like that. Oh, yes…" And then she eased her legs apart, the signal he was waiting for, her body's assurance that she wanted more.

He was only too happy to give her more. He touched her intimately, parting her.

She was wet and open. She spoke against his mouth. "Oh, Travis. Please…" She rocked her hips into his touch. He caressed her more deeply.

And then he eased one leg between her thighs. She gasped—and moved her sleek thighs even wider apart. He settled himself between them, carefully, doing his best to distribute his weight so he didn't crush her beneath him.

No, she wasn't the kind of woman he could easily crush. But still, he didn't want her to feel smothered or hemmed in or overpowered. Not in any way.

Only then did he lift his mouth from hers. Her eyelids fluttered open. She looked at him, her gaze glazed and hungry.

"Touch me," he whispered. "You set the pace."

She didn't hesitate. She reached down between them and took him gently in her hand. She guided him home.

He braced up on his elbows to get more control. And in an agony of slowness, he pressed in.

Little by little, he entered her. Pushing in a fraction, holding still, watching her flushed face for any sign that she didn't welcome him, that he might be hurting her.

But she only lifted toward him. She wrapped her arms around him, whispered, "Yes, it's good. More..."

At last, he filled her. Her body stretched and gave around him. They were together in the most complete way.

She rocked her hips up to him.

He held still, letting her take him, do what she would with him, letting her set her own pace. It was pure torture, to hold back so she could lead the way.

Pure torture, but in a really good way.

She lifted up, took his mouth again, plunged her hot, wet tongue inside.

He knew then. She was okay with this. More than okay.

Her sweet, strong body called to him. He couldn't help but answer. He rocked his hips toward her. She rose to meet him.

And after that, he was lost in sweet, consuming heat. He let go and let it happen.

The world spun away and it was only him and Sam and this miracle of pleasure that burned so hot and bright between them. There was only her kiss and the magical scent of her, the feel of her beneath him, rocking him hard and fast, holding on so tight as they rose to touch the stars.

Sam was a happy woman.

Truly happy.

Yeah, okay. Part of it was the sex. After she got past her own fears and awkwardness, it had been terrific. Better than she'd ever dreamed it might be. But also, well, she believed Travis when he said he wouldn't let the past ruin what they'd found together. The nagging worry that something wasn't right with him receded.

She could just enjoy being with him.

And she did. They spent Tuesday at the ranch. Tuesday night, they went to Armadillo Rose, the San Antonio bar owned by Matt's wife, Corrine. Davis and Aleta had volunteered to stay behind and watch the children. The three younger couples—Elena and Rogan, Mercy and Luke, and Sam and Travis—rode into San Antonio in Rogan's SUV.

Armadillo Rose, which had been owned by Corrine's mother before her, was a funky, fun place with loud music and cute bartenders in skimpy tops and cowboy boots.

Corrine had pitchers of margaritas brought to their table, and Asher, Travis's oldest brother, and his wife, Tessa, joined them. A few minutes later, Matt showed up. And then Marnie and Jericho, too.

They played pool. Corrine even took a break to take on Sam. Sam won that time, two out of three.

It was a family party in more ways than one. Not only were five of the seven Bravo brothers there, but Marnie and Tessa—like Elena and Mercy—were sisters. Before Marnie married Jericho and Tessa said "I do" to Ash, their last name had been Jones.

Marnie told funny stories of growing up in the wild, woolly Jones clan in a tiny town in the California Sierras. She and Tessa had a crazy old grandpa named Oggie and a stepmother they adored. Tessa said that their dad had been a wild man until he settled down with their kind and loving stepmother. They also had two much younger half brothers who, Marnie announced, were born to carry on the Jones tradition of generally raising holy hell.

Sam could so relate. She ended up telling a few stories about her dad, who had a real thing for fireworks. She even revealed his nickname, Ted the Torch. Every Fourth of July, he insisted on buying every bottle rocket and firecracker he could get his hands on. Twice he'd been cited and had to pay whopping fines for setting off fireworks where fireworks weren't allowed.

The five couples and Matt stayed to close up the place. It was raining as Rogan drove them home, a misty kind of rain. Sam and Travis sat in the rear seat. She rested her head on his shoulder and watched the jeweled drops speckle the windshield up in front and thought that she had never in her life felt so…accepted.

Not only was Travis as gone on her as she was on him, but she also adored his family. His brothers were the greatest. And his sisters and sisters-in-law, well, Sam liked them all. They were good people. It seemed like a hundred years ago that she had worried they might look down on her.

A little while later, alone in their rooms, Travis showed her again how good it could be when a woman found the right man.

Wednesday morning, Irina, Caleb's wife, called. She invited Travis and Sam to dinner that night. Because they were going to San Antonio in the evening anyway, she and Travis decided to spend the day in town, just the two of them.

They toured the Alamo in the morning.

Travis told her that his mom sometimes worked as a tour guide there. And that before he said he was engaged to Sam, Aleta had been planning to set him up with another tour guide named Ashley.

Sam couldn't resist teasing him. "Maybe we should ask if Ashley's giving the tour today...."

He put an arm around her and pulled her close. "Don't even think about it." He kissed her then, a quick, possessive kiss that made her breath catch in her throat. It was a revelation to her. How just being with him made every moment so full, so exciting. He spoke again in a low growl. "Keep looking at me like that and I won't be responsible for my behavior."

"That was my plan." She leaned her head on his shoulder. It didn't get any better than this. To be with him in the truest way, held close in the warm circle of his arm.

Their tour guide, as it turned out, was a tall, slim, balding man named Otis. He spoke eloquently of the history of the Alamo, explaining that it had been built as Mission San Antonio del Valero, one of five missions along San Antonio's Mission Trail. Otis went on to tell the old story with feeling, all about how, in 1836, 189 Texan soldiers bravely defended the fort for thirteen days before finally being massacred by six thousand of Santa Anna's troops.

After the Alamo, they had lunch at a great Mexican restaurant and bakery in Market Square. When they'd finished the meal and the waiter had cleared off their plates, Travis took her left hand across the table.

He rubbed his thumb across the big diamond on the ring he'd bought her. "It looks good on you. Really good."

She squeezed his hand. "I love it. I do. And I have to be careful."

He tipped his head to the side, frowning. "Be careful of what?"

"Well, I mean, lately, I could almost forget that this

isn't really my engagement ring, that we're not really engaged."

He brought her hand to his mouth, brushed his lips across her fingers. The touch of his mouth on her skin made her think of their nights together, made her wish for a thousand more of them. "It feels real to me, too." He lowered her fingers to the table again, put his other hand over hers, covering the bright diamond, enclosing her hand in both of his. "I want us to *make* it real."

Her heart stuttered in her chest, and then began racing. "Um, Travis?"

"Yeah?" His eyes gleamed.

"Did you just ask me to marry you?"

Chapter Ten

Instead of answering her question, he said, "Wait, I should be on my knees, right?" Which, she realized, *was* the answer to her question.

She gripped his hand, embarrassed. Thrilled. Blown away. "Oh, no, really? Right here in the restaurant?"

"Absolutely." He was off his chair and on one knee before she could stop him.

A guy at a nearby table remarked, "Now, that's the way you do it."

Somebody else applauded.

Travis still held her hand in both of his. And he said with feeling, "Sam, it's you. You're the one for me. Say yes."

She looked down into his eyes. And she thought how this was exactly what she'd dreamed of, what she'd longed for, in her secret heart—even when she hadn't dared to admit that a life with Travis was what she wanted more than anything.

At the same time, an unwelcome voice in the back of her mind whispered, *Whoa, slow down. This is happening way too fast.*

Sam closed her mind to that voice, to her doubts. She had everything now. She *was* the woman she'd always believed she had no chance of ever being. And Travis wanted her for his wife.

He wanted her for real, not just because his mom wouldn't get off his back.

He was offering her what she'd always yearned for. No frickin' way she was turning him down.

"Sam." He looked up at her with such hopeful tenderness. "Help me out here. Give me an answer. The right answer. Say yes. Please."

She knew half the restaurant was listening in now. Even the waiters had stopped to watch.

The annoying voice echoed in her head again. *He knows you won't put the brakes on. Not here. In a public place. He knows you could never embarrass him that way....*

No.

That wasn't true.

It was only the voice of her doubts, the voice of her insecurities, the voice of the lonely girl she used to be. She wasn't letting that voice stop her from grabbing her happiness with both hands.

"Sam?" Did he sound worried now?

She couldn't stand that. "Yes!" She laughed—in nervousness and in joy. "Yes, of course. You know that. Yes."

He swept to his feet, pulling her with him, and gathered her into his arms. Everyone in the restaurant seemed to be clapping. "You had me worried there for a minute," he whispered.

"Sorry. You kind of caught me by surprise."

"It's okay. I forgive you because you gave me the answer I was looking for. Kiss me, Sam."

She didn't hesitate that time. She kissed him with all the love and longing she'd been holding in her heart.

Just for him.

For way too long.

At Caleb's house that evening they held hands underneath the table.

Irina beamed at them. "Love. It makes the world go round and round." Her gaze strayed to Caleb and they shared an intimate glance.

Who knew? Sam found herself thinking. What had started out as a lie had ended up becoming the truth. The beautiful, amazing, absolute truth.

Engaged to Travis. If someone had told her two weeks ago that Travis would take a knee in the middle of a restaurant and propose to her for real, she would have laughed and said, "No way. Never. Not a chance."

So much for all her old assumptions.

She had conquered her worst fears—that she wasn't quite good enough, wasn't woman enough, didn't have enough class. And as a result, she had won her prince.

And speaking of princes...

Sam met a real one that night. His name was Rule.

Prince Rule Bravo DeCalibretti. He was a cousin to the Bravos, the second-born son of one of Davis's long-lost brothers. Born in Montedoro, a tiny principality on the Mediterranean, His Highness was visiting America for the second time. Rule said he enjoyed getting to know his father's country a little. Rule was tall and dark and handsome, as all princes should be. He was staying with Gabe and Mary Bravo and would be coming out to Bravo Ridge tomorrow to celebrate Thanksgiving—that most American of holidays—with the San Antonio branch of the family.

And Rule wasn't the only royalty there that night. Irina was a princess. Seriously. Or she would have been, if things had been different. There was actually a book about Irina's life. A big, fat one, with lots of glossy pictures. Sam thumbed through it, thoroughly amazed. Irina didn't seem the least unhappy that she would never be a queen. She was the picture of contentment living in San Antonio with the husband she adored and their gorgeous little daughter.

Sam and Travis left Caleb's at a little after eleven. They were back at the ranch before midnight.

Holding hands, they climbed the stairs to the rooms they shared. He took her in his arms the minute they shut the door behind them.

"I wanted to tell them all tonight," he whispered. "That we're together. That you're really mine."

"But they wouldn't have understood." She brushed a butterfly-light kiss across his mouth. "Because they all think we were already engaged."

He claimed another kiss, a longer, deeper one. And as he kissed her, he took hold of her sweater and eased it up over her ribcage. She raised her arms. They broke the kiss long enough for him to pull the sweater over her head. He reclaimed her mouth and he turned her, continuing the kiss, and waltzed her backward to the bed. They fell across it together.

He lifted away enough to add, "And if I told them that I asked you to marry me today and you said yes, then I would have had to explain everything…."

She touched his cheek, already scratchy from a day's

worth of beard. "It'll make a good story, one of these days."

He smiled. "Something to tell our kids, when they think we're old and boring."

"Our kids…" She considered that possibility. "I never thought…you and me. Kids." She nudged off her shoes, heard them plunk to the bedside rug.

"Well, think about it now," he said gruffly, sitting up to get rid of his own sweater. "Because it's going to happen."

"And I'm so glad." She pushed him back down and leaned over him, laying her hand on his chest, which was so wonderfully broad and deep and heavy with muscle.

Another kiss. She caressed him, running the backs of her fingers along the side of his neck. Then she pushed away and sat up.

He caught her arm. "Where do you think you're going?"

She gave a lazy shrug. "Well, I *was* going to help you with your boots…."

"Ah." He let her go, lay back and folded his hands behind his head. "In that case, okay." He held up a boot.

Shaking her head, she slid off the bed, braced her feet on the rug, took the heel in one hand and the toe in the other and pulled. The boot slid off easily. She took the other one off, too, and his socks as well, while she was at it. Then she stretched out beside him again.

Idly, he traced the line of her hair where it curled against her temple. And then he let his finger glide lower, around the line of her jaw, down the jut of her chin, the length of her throat. He lingered for a moment or two at her collarbones, tracing one and then the other. He laid his warm palm against her upper chest. It felt so good there, so right.

Finally, he skimmed the top of her low-cut satin bra, making her sigh.

With his gaze, he followed the slow progress of that skimming finger. "With you here, I really feel I'm… coming home at last, you know?" His voice was touched with roughness and desire. He glanced up again and their eyes met.

She scanned his face. It was a good face, the kind of face she would never tire of looking at. "I'm glad, Travis. So glad…"

A slight frown creased his brow. "What would you think about moving here?"

The question surprised her. She rose up on an elbow. "South Texas Oil has something for you here, in San Antonio?"

"Not STOI. BravoCorp."

BravoCorp. The family business. Davis was president and chairman of the board. Caleb was the top sales rep, Gabe the company attorney, Matt CFO and Ash CEO. BravoCorp invested in any number of different projects. Once they'd been mostly in land development, but with the economic downturn, they'd diversified. Now, they had various investments they managed all over the country, in Spain and in South America. Also, for as long as she'd known Travis, they'd put a good chunk of their capital into oil.

She took a not-so-wild guess. "They still want you to take over the family oil interests?" He'd mentioned in the past that he could always have a place in the family business. He'd just never wanted that before.

He rubbed her shoulder, caressed the length of her arm. "My dad brought it up yesterday. And Gabe mentioned the idea again tonight. I would be vice president in charge of petroleum exploration and development."

"Whoa. Way impressive."

"The money would be really good, a big salary, great benefits and a strong bonus structure." He named an eye-popping figure.

"Wow."

He was watching her closely. "Say it," he grumbled.

"Oh, come on. You know what I'm thinking."

"So come out with it."

"Well, you've always said you wanted to make your own way."

"I see things differently now. We're getting married. We want to have kids, so coming home to stay, being near the family, it suddenly has a big appeal."

"I can understand that." She also experienced a certain...wariness. That feeling she'd had in the restaurant, when he proposed, that they were moving awfully fast, talking about changing everything up when she'd barely gotten used to the astonishing fact that they were together and they both wanted to stay that way.

It wasn't that changing things was bad. She'd been making some changes herself after all. It was only... well, he surprised her. All of a sudden, he was talking about going to work with his family when he'd never been the least willing to consider such a thing before.

He touched the flare of her hip. She shivered a little in anticipation of the other places he might touch. Her apprehensions faded as desire bloomed.

And then he said, "We could get our own place here, in San Antonio. A really nice place in a great neighborhood. Since you're not taking another job offshore anyway, you could just take a hiatus for a while."

Her misgiving came creeping back. "A hiatus? From?"

"Work."

She just didn't get it. "But, Travis, I want to work."

"I put that wrong. Because you *would* be working. It's a full-time job, to be a mother. To raise a family."

"Well, yes, I can see that. I get that. But I told you, I want to get my degree, get a new job…"

"But there's no hurry to do that. It's not like with kids."

"What do you mean?"

"You're thirty years old, Sam."

"Well, yeah. And I—"

"Sam." He didn't wait for her to finish. "We need to get on with having those kids we've been talking about. You know that we do. And you need to be…safe, most of all."

What did he mean by that? "Safe from what, exactly?"

He wasn't looking at her.

She touched his face. And then she had to wait several seconds before he turned her way and she could see his eyes. "Safe?"

He didn't answer right way. But then, gruffly, he confessed, "I wouldn't make it. I couldn't do that again. If something happened to you…"

"Travis." She laid her palm against his beard-scratchy cheek, held it there, a touch meant to comfort, to reassure. "What happened to Rachel, you know that was a one-in-a-million thing. One of those things that could happen to anyone. Not something you could have protected her against."

"Not true. If I had been there, it might have been different."

"What? You were going to stick by her side every minute of every day?"

"Don't exaggerate."

"I'm not. It's just, well, life itself is frickin' hazardous. No one gets out alive."

He glared at her. "You know what I mean, Sam." And then he softened his tone. "We just have to be more careful, you know?"

She really, really did not like this. "You're not making sense. Are you telling me I'm not supposed to walk across the street by myself?"

His eyes were so dark, so determined. "I can protect you. I *will* protect you."

"Travis, that's just not realistic. Some things you can't protect another person against."

"You can't know that. You can never know that. There's always something a man can do so that the bad stuff can be prevented."

She could see that she needed to try a different tack with this. "Look at it this way."

"What way?" He didn't look the least receptive.

She refused to give up. "I've done a very dangerous job for over a decade. And see?" She gestured down the length of her body. "All in one piece, in perfect health."

He still wasn't buying. "You're purposely misunderstanding me."

"No." She searched his face. "I'm not. Honestly, I'm not."

"I want us to get married right away." He spoke so intently. Heatedly. "I want to buy a house. And I want to have kids."

She realized she had to say it right out loud. "Look, you're…moving awfully fast, don't you think? Maybe too fast?"

There. She had said it. Spoken her concern out loud.

And she instantly saw that it had done her no good.

He refused to understand. "Fast?" He growled the word. And then he sat up and swung his feet to the floor.

"Travis…" She tried to catch his arm. He only shrugged off her touch as he stood. "Travis, come on…"

He ignored her plea and moved on silent feet to the window. He stared out on the dark side yard, his broad, bare back set against her. "What do you mean fast? I thought we were both agreed about what we wanted, about how it would be."

"Well, I just…" She tried to frame an answer, to explain how his beautiful proposal that afternoon had happened so quickly, given that they'd been lovers for only a couple of days—quickly, and also like something of a manipulation, made right out in public like that, where putting him off would have shamed him.

But she didn't want to go there if she didn't have to. Because it *had* been a great moment. And she *did* want to marry him, to have children with him. It was a wonder and a miracle to her, that she'd finally found what for so long had been only a distant dream to her.

But her frustration was mounting. "You know, the least you can do is look at me when I'm talking to you."

Slowly, he turned and faced her again. "We finally found each other. *Really* found each other. This is our chance. Why can't you see that?" His eyes were shadowed, but he spoke with such passion. Somehow, that gave her hope. They did want the same things. He just wanted everything right now. She was more cautious. She just didn't see why they needed to rush.

Lowering her feet to the rug, she rose to her height. "Oh, Travis, please." She went to him. He watched her approach, his jaw set, his eyes flaring to anger again. She halted a foot away from him. Somehow, it didn't seem safe to get closer. "I know it's our chance. I agree with you. I'm so happy that we're together now."

"Right," he spoke with a clear edge of sarcasm. "So happy you refuse to let me take care of you."

She kept her head high, her voice low and even. "But you can't just ask me to give up all my dreams. To suddenly, overnight, be someone I'm not."

"Someone you're not." He repeated her words, heavy on the irony. "So what you're really telling me is that you don't want to marry me?"

"I never said that. Of course I want to marry you."

"You don't want to have kids, then."

"Yes. Yes, I do. I love you and want to marry you and have kids with you. I also want to go back to college and finish getting my degree—and then find a job that works for me. It's the twenty-first century, Travis. I don't see why I can't do all those things."

"I didn't say you couldn't. I said there had to be priorities."

She took a slow, careful breath. "And your priorities are?"

"I told you. I want to move ahead with our plans. I want to have a baby right away. Maybe your going to college and getting started on that new career will have to take a back seat for a while."

"What you mean is that you want to move ahead with *your* plans and *my* plans will have to wait."

"Marriage and children," he said flatly. "That's my plan. You told me a minute ago that you wanted that, too."

"I do."

He made a low, angry sound. Raising a hand, his bicep flexing powerfully, he raked his fingers back through his hair in a gesture that spoke all too clearly of his exasperation with her.

They'd reached an impasse. She got that. She hadn't spent all her working life dealing with men and finding ways to break through stalemates not to recognize a deadlock when she saw one.

Someone had to give. She very much doubted that that someone would be Travis.

At work, she always tried to figure out the deeper problem in a situation like this, to get down to what was holding the other guy back from working with her and moving forward, and also to admit to whatever her own issues were. Sometimes the root problem would be something as simple as the need to be right.

A man hated to be wrong—well, so did a woman. But for a man, especially, being right seemed keyed into the drive to survive. Men had a basic need to protect others—women and children most of all. And to protect others they had to make the right decisions. They often held on to bad decisions because they couldn't stand to face the simple fact that they'd been wrong in a judgment call, that they hadn't been effective protectors.

Protection.

What had he said a few minutes ago? *I can protect you. I* will *protect you....*

Yeah, that was the key here. He wanted to protect her. He wanted to make sure that what had happened to Rachel could never happen to her. He *needed* to believe that he *could* protect her against accidents of fate—even though what he needed to believe just wasn't true.

"What?" he demanded. "Why are you looking at me like that?"

Where to even begin? "Travis, I..." He waited, glaring. She made herself continue. "I think that we need to…talk about Rachel."

His face was set against her. "What for? This has nothing to do with Rachel."

"I think it does—or at least, it has to do with what happened to Rachel. And what that did to *you*." She held out her hand. With some reluctance, he took it. "Come on." She pulled him back toward the bed. He went— dragging his feet a little, yeah. But he went. She sat on the edge of the mattress and pulled him down beside her.

He sat with the same lack of enthusiasm he'd shown for giving her his hand. "Okay," he grumbled. "Say it, whatever it is."

She twined her fingers with his. "It wasn't your fault that Rachel died."

"I know that." He shook his head. "I'm not a child, Sam." He spoke more in reproach than in anger. She decided to take that as a good sign.

"Well, all right." She bumped her shoulder against his, squeezed his fingers. "Just checkin'." She slanted him a glance and saw he was looking at her.

His gaze had turned softer. "Sam…" His voice was softer, too. "It's like some miracle, you and me. I never thought I would be willing, you know, to…go there again. To take a chance on losing everything all over again."

"I know. I do remember how much you loved Rachel."

"I couldn't…make it work, with Wanda."

"I know."

His eyes had changed again. They were far away now. "I thought I could. But she just…wasn't Rachel. I would look at her and wonder how I got there with her. I realized too late that she wasn't the one for me. I wanted to prove to myself I was over Rachel. So I asked Wanda to marry me—and then I never really gave her a chance. I drove her away, into that other guy's open arms."

Sam made a low noise in her throat. But she didn't speak. This was, after all, for him to say.

And then he was looking at her again, really *seeing* her. "But with you...it's so good with you. Partly because we were friends for all those years first, I think. You really changed things up during that week with Jonathan. And I finally saw you as a woman. All woman. But you're still Sam, still the same person I've always known. I don't think of Rachel—or of anyone else— when I look at you. I just see...you. You're *all* that I see." He pulled his hand from hers—but only to wrap those gentle fingers around the back of her neck and pull her close for a slow, tender kiss.

When they came up for air, she whispered, "I feel the same about you. Oh, Travis. You're everything to me. I want us to work this out, to find a way that we both get what we want. We can't...do that if you're pushing too hard, if you're trying to make me into someone I'm not."

He pressed his forehead to hers. "I get that. I do."

"You can't...protect me absolutely. There is no such thing as absolute safety. We're *not* safe in life. The best we can do is try to be a little bit wise, and a little bit careful. And brave. We need to be brave."

He rubbed his cheek against hers, his beard stubble creating a slight, lovely friction. "Yes, ma'am."

Had she actually gotten through to him? She did hope so. "So you'll stop...pushing me?"

He cradled her face in his hands. "I just want us to be married."

"Okay. I get that. I want to be married to you, too. But I also plan to go ahead with my education, to get my degree and—"

"You said that. I get it."

Did he? She wasn't sure. She wanted to find a way to pin him down about it.

But another thing she'd learned through all the years of doing a man's job—you didn't beat an issue to death with a man. You could lose whatever ground you might have gained if you kept after him too long. Sometimes you just had to table the discussion and come back to go at it again another day.

It was a process she'd never particularly enjoyed.

"Sam?" He nuzzled her ear, nipped at her earlobe.

Down below, she felt that wonderful, warm weakness. "Yeah?"

"Marry me."

A low laugh escaped her. "Wait a minute, didn't I already say that I would?"

"I mean let's set the date. Let's go for it."

She gulped—and started to feel railroaded again.

But then she stopped herself. It wasn't the wedding that she had a problem with. It wasn't being Travis's wife. She *wanted* to be his wife, she truly did. "You... have a date in mind?"

"December. The third Saturday, I think."

"Uh. December. As in next month? A few weeks away...?"

"That's it," he said softly. Why did that seem like much too soon? She wasn't even sure yet that they had an understanding, that he wouldn't be pressuring her constantly to stay home, to get pregnant ASAP, to give up college and her plans for a new career. He took her chin, guided it around so she looked in his eyes. "I was thinking we could get married here, at Bravo Ridge."

"Here?" she echoed weakly, still trying to get her mind around the enormity of the step they would be taking.

He nodded. "My mom would be thrilled to help in any way she could. She'll make sure the wedding is exactly the way you want it. We could invite the families—yours and mine. And any friends you want to be there and even some of the guys we've worked with over the years, if you want."

She was scared to death. Which probably proved that Travis wasn't the only one with emotional issues here.

Oh, yeah. Definitely. Setting the date was freaking her out.

And yet, well...

What he suggested sounded pretty much perfect. It did. Just the kind of wedding she would want if she was going to have one. Small and comfortable. The family. And a few good friends.

Strange. To think of herself as a bride. But kind of nice, too.

Still, she hesitated to say yes. It didn't feel right to her. And she couldn't decide whether it didn't feel right because he was pushing her again—or if the problem actually was hers.

She'd been on her own for so long, answerable to no one but herself. Being married—even to Travis, even if he backed off on his sudden campaign to make her into his happy little homemaker—well, it was pretty frickin' huge. It really was.

Getting married would change her life even more completely than she'd been planning on changing it.

Was she ready for that?

He spoke again. "You talked about Rachel…."

"Yeah?"

"Well, one thing I always wished I'd done differently…"

"Yeah?"

"I just wish we'd been married, you know, Rachel and me? If it had to happen, if I had to lose her, I wish we had been married first. I wish, just for a day or two, she might have been my wife." He shut his eyes. Made a low, pained sound deep in his throat. "God, I can't believe I said that." He shook his head. "I mean, she died. What the hell did it really matter, whether I ever called her my wife?"

Tenderly, she told him, "It mattered to you, Travis. It mattered a lot."

He blew out a breath and muttered, "Now you'll think I'm a complete wuss."

"Uh-uh. No, I don't think that. Never. I think you're brave and good and…true at heart. That's what I think, Travis Bravo. That's what I *know*."

"Then say yes, Sam," he whispered. "Say yes to you and me."

And when he put it that way, well, her heart melted. When he put it that way, what else could she say but, "Yeah, all right."

He took both her hands in his and he sat back from her a little. His eyes were bright as stars. "Say that again."

She swallowed down the lump in her throat and she said it right out loud. "Let's get married, Travis. Let's do this thing. Let's do it here, at Bravo Ridge. On the third Saturday in December."

Chapter Eleven

Travis kissed her. For a long time.

And then he said, "Tomorrow at dinner we'll tell them all that we've set the date."

"Oh, Travis…" She shook her head.

His gaze grew wary. She saw worry there, that she would find some way to put him off. "Why not?"

"Tomorrow your mom and dad reaffirm their vows."

"So?"

"Well, it should be *their* day, don't you think? I'd rather talk to your mom about it on Friday—and Mercy, too. I mean, it's her house. Shouldn't we ask her if she's up for having our wedding here?"

"There's no need to ask her. She'll be fine with it."

"I just think it's the right thing to do, you know? To talk to your mom and Mercy first."

He looked at her for a long time. Finally, he said, "I have to ask…."

"What?"

"Are you stalling me?"

"No, I'm not. I promise I'm not." She was proud of how open and sincere she sounded. Even though maybe she *was* stalling. Just a little.

But he seemed to believe her. Slowly, he nodded. "All right. But first thing Friday morning, we'll—no. Wait a minute. Friday's the big shopping thing, right? You, Mom, Elena and Mercy will be out of here before dawn."

Black Friday. She'd totally forgotten. "Well, yeah. But we won't be out shopping forever."

"Trust me. I know how Black Friday goes. It will last until three or four in the afternoon. At least."

"So then, we'll talk to your mom and Mercy as soon as we get back."

He held her gaze. "Friday afternoon, then. When you get back here to the ranch…"

"Absolutely."

"I'm holding you to that."

"Travis, come on. I won't let you down."

"Say that again."

"I won't…" Her words trailed off as he laid the pad of a finger against her lips.

"On second thought," he said softly, "don't tell me. Show me."

Davis and Aleta reaffirmed their marriage vows at one in the afternoon on Thanksgiving Day in the big living room there at the ranch, surrounded by their children. And their children's children.

Sam, who never let anyone see her cry, found herself kind of misty-eyed over the whole thing. Davis was handsome and imposing as always, in a fine gray-striped suit, silver-gray silk shirt and blue tie. Aleta looked like a bride again, in a cream-colored silk shirt-dress that flattered her slim figure.

When they shared the kiss that reaffirmed their life-long commitment to each other, Sam wasn't the only with tears in her eyes.

Later, they all sat down at the long table in the dining room to share Thanksgiving dinner.

Aleta said, kind of shyly, "I have written a special grace, just for this special day."

Davis, looking pretty choked up, cleared his throat and said somberly, "Let's bow our heads."

Everyone did, even the little ones.

And Aleta's gentle voice filled the high-ceilinged room. "We thank you, Lord, for this day, for this fine meal laid before us, for all of us, together. For the ties that bind us, the ties that hold us, heart to heart. We are ever grateful for your understanding. And for your patience as we slowly come to learn and accept our own failings—and then overcome them. As we find what really matters in this life—the love we share. The love we give. The love we always find waiting, strong and abiding, when we are so very sure there is no hope. On this day made for thankfulness, we are grateful beyond measure. Thank you. Amen."

"Amen!" crowed little Lucas. "Amen, amen, amen!"

Smiling, lifting their heads again, everyone said it, "Amen."

That night, as soon as they were alone in their rooms, Travis pulled Sam close. "I talked to Mom about the wedding."

The muscles between her shoulder blades jerked

tight, but she was careful to keep her voice neutral. "When was that?"

"I got her alone for a few minutes just now. And I talked to Mercy, too."

"I wondered where you'd gone off to." She eased free of his embrace and went to the windows.

"Sam..." He came to her, put his hands on her shoulders. Warmth spiraled down inside her. She was a total sucker for his lightest touch. He spoke softly, coaxingly. "I told Mom I knew I was out of line to ask her now, that I'd promised you we'd wait until tomorrow so that today could be all about her and dad."

"And she said...?"

"She said what a wonderful woman you are."

Sam made a humphing sound and kept her back to him. "Yeah, right. What else was she going to say?"

"You have to know she was thrilled. Why wouldn't she be? This is what she's been waiting for. The last of her kids, finally making the leap. She said she was so happy for us. And that she'd be glad to help in any way she could. And she meant it. And Mercy told me she was honored that we wanted to have the wedding here. It's getting to be a family tradition. Mercy and Luke got married here, at the ranch. And so did Elena and Rogan."

Sam shook her head and kept her gaze on the distant, silvery moon. "We had an agreement."

"Sam." He turned her to face him. "You're right. I should have waited, like we agreed. I'm sorry, okay?" He looked at her so hopefully. "Forgive me?"

She wanted to stay annoyed at him.

Which was kind of petty, the more she thought about it—petty, and also dishonest. Because she *had* been stalling, even though she kept telling him that she wasn't.

She started thinking about how far they'd come. Friends. To lovers. To so much more.

So okay. She was scared. Of her own insecurities. Of the past that hadn't really let him go.

But holding a grudge because he hadn't kept to the letter of some minor agreement would do neither of them any good.

She went into his waiting arms and rested her head in the crook of his shoulder. "You're forgiven."

"Good." His deep voice rumbled under her ear. He stroked her hair.

It would be all right, she told herself. They would make it work, together, create a good life, the two of them.

She sighed and snuggled closer.

He lifted her chin for a kiss.

The next morning, long before dawn, taking care not to wake her sleeping fiancé, Sam eased back the blankets, slipped her feet to the rug and tiptoed from bed.

She met Mercy, Elena and Aleta downstairs. They drove into San Antonio, to Tessa's house, where the rest of the women of the family were gathered.

In two vehicles, they caravanned to North Star Mall. And they shopped without a single break until well past noon.

It was Sam's very first Black Friday experience. She bought presents for everyone on her Christmas list—which had grown considerably since she'd come to San Antonio. The stores were crowded. It was a total zoo.

Before Jonathan, she never would have lasted an hour

in the hordes of eager, mostly women shoppers. She would have run screaming for the parking lot.

She made a mental note to call Jonathan and thank him. She even bought him a rhinestone-studded set of suspenders at Saks Fifth Avenue and had them gift-wrapped in festive green and red. He would probably hate them. They weren't tasteful in the least.

But she didn't care. She knew that even if he looked down his fashion-forward nose at them, he would love that she had gone out and found them just for him.

At lunch, the talk was all about how Sam and Travis had set the date. Everyone said they'd be there, at the ranch, for the ceremony and the family party after.

They shopped some more.

Sam took a break around two. She wandered out of Dillard's, her arms full of packages, and dropped gratefully onto a sofa in a sitting area next to a Christmas tree. Aleta emerged from the same store a couple of minutes later. Sam called her over and scooted down enough to make a place for her.

They sat together, listening to the endless loop of piped-in Christmas music, watching a couple of toddlers chase each other around the tree, laughing, stumbling, falling—and then picking themselves right up and chasing each other some more.

Aleta was smiling. "Every year I tell myself I really don't need to put myself through the Black Friday experience again. And then every year when Zoe or Mercy or Tessa or Corrine insists I come with them, well, I just can't say no. And this is the first year we've all gone together. I have to say, it's been great."

Sam tipped her head back and took in the giant gold bell tied with a ginormous red bow suspended above their heads. "I have loved every minute of it," she said, and meant it. "Even though I have to tell you. My feet are killing me."

"Oh, honey..." Aleta put her hand over Sam's. "You have no idea." *Honey.* It was what Travis's mom called her own children. And her daughters-in-law. Sam got the total warm-and-fuzzies at that moment. She felt accepted. Loved, even. Aleta really was an amazing person. She had a truly generous heart. She leaned a little closer to Sam. "And speaking of shopping, we must find you your wedding dress soon. There's not a lot of time to waste."

Sam laughed, though deep inside apprehension stirred. "Blame Travis. He wants to get married and get married now."

"And you don't?"

Sam met Aleta's clear blue eyes. "I admit I wanted to wait awhile. It's all happening so fast with us."

The faint lines between Aleta's brows deepened. "But you've known each other for so long."

Sam glanced away. "True."

Aleta squeezed her hand. "And you seem so happy together."

"We are. It's just...oh, I don't know...."

"Did you want a big wedding? So many girls do. If you do, we can—"

Sam groaned. "Oh, please God. No."

"You just feel...rushed?"

"A little. I..." Sam let her voice trail off. She knew she never should have started this conversation.

There was just too much that Travis's sweet mom didn't know for Aleta to be able to understand Sam's doubts and concerns. Maybe someday, Sam would tell Aleta everything. About the Sam she had been, the Sam she'd suddenly become with the help of Travis's trust fund and her own personal fairy godmother. About the fake engagement that had magically become real. About Travis and his need to make her his wife, now, immediately, the way he hadn't done with Rachel. But today, at the mall, in the middle of the Black Friday shop-a-thon? Uh-uh. Not the right time.

Plus, well, it seemed disloyal to Travis, to tell Aleta that they'd pretended to be engaged because she wouldn't stop throwing women at him. She needed Travis's go-ahead to get into that.

And was any of it information Aleta actually needed? No. What mattered to her was that Sam and Travis were together, that her prodigal son had come home at last.

Aleta made a worried sound. "It's a big step, getting married. And it's not unheard-of for a bride to have some misgivings. But if you really feel it's too soon…"

"No." She put on a bright smile. "I want to marry Travis. So much. I honestly do."

"But honey, you said you feel rushed."

"Only a little."

"You're sure?"

"I am positive." She said it so firmly that she almost believed it. "This wedding—at the ranch, with you and the whole family there—it's just the kind of wedding I've always dreamed of."

"You can talk to me. I want you to know that. Any time you need a sounding board, or just someone to listen."

"Thanks, Aleta. I'll remember that."

Aleta shifted beside her, bending to pull her packages closer at her feet. "Will you invite your mother to your wedding?"

"I was thinking I would, yeah. And my stepfather. And my wicked half sisters, too." Not that they would come.

Aleta was chuckling. "Oh, your sisters are wicked, are they?"

"Not really. But…"

"What? Tell me."

Sam sighed. "They are a couple of snobby little twits."

"Twits, huh?"

"Well, they're a lot younger than me. And we never really got along. They're twins, did I mention that?"

"You did, yes. That first day you arrived."

"Dina and Mila. They're fifteen now. I haven't seen them in a couple of years." The last time had not been fun. The two had whispered about her behind their tiny little hands and giggled every time she entered a room where they happened to be.

"I'm glad you're inviting them," Aleta said. "And your father…?"

"Well, I've been meaning to warn you about him."

Aleta faked a look of alarm. "I need a warning?"

"He's a crusty old guy. And his girlfriend, Keisha, is younger than I am. They live in a Winnebago. So the Winnebago would be coming to the wedding, too."

"The Winnebago is welcome."

"Well, I'm just saying. My family is a little odd."

"If they're *your* family, they're *our* family."

Sam shook her head. "I think you should wait until you meet them to make that call."

Sam phoned her mom the next morning.

"Samantha, how wonderful," Jennifer Early Jaworski Carlson said when she heard the news. "Of course I will be there. And Walt and your sisters would love to come, too."

"Uh. Well, great, Mom." Sam felt slightly shell-shocked. She'd never for a second expected her mom to say yes. Let alone announce she was bringing Walt and the Terrible Twins. "Have you got a pencil?"

"Right here." Her mom repeated the date that Sam had already mentioned.

"That's it." Sam gave her the address and phone number of the ranch. "And Mercy—that's Travis's sister-in-law—has said you're welcome to stay here, at Bravo Ridge, if that works for you."

"How kind of her. I'll talk to Walt. See if he wants to drive down, or if we'll fly—and I'll call within the next couple of days and let you know if we'll be taking your fiancé's sister-in-law up on her thoughtful invitation."

"Well, okay. Great. Terrific, then."

"*You're* getting married," said her mother wonderingly. As if she'd never in million years thought *that* would happen. Sam tried not to feel defensive. But her mom had a habit of giving her grief about how she needed to dress up now then, how it wouldn't hurt to be just a little bit feminine. How a man appreciated a woman who *acted* like a woman. Around her mother and her mother's family, Sam had always felt like a freak—and an oversize one at that. "What about your dress? I'll help you with that. Come on up to Minneapolis and I'll take you shopping."

"Thanks, Mom, but I've got it handled."

"You're *certain?*" Her mom's complete lack of faith in Sam's ability to choose her own wedding dress was not the least flattering—even if, until Jonathan, her mom would have been right.

"I'm positive. I'll find my own dress." Sam made a few more polite noises and said goodbye as fast as she could after that.

Travis, fresh from the shower, wearing only a pair of snug faded jeans and looking like an invitation to sin, appeared in the door to the blue bedroom. "Your mom?" At her nod, he grinned. "You should see your face."

She blinked and shook her head. "They're coming to the wedding. All four of them."

"Good for them."

"Hah. Easy for you to say. Wait until you meet them. They're everything I've ever told you they were. And more—or should I say *less?* They're all so tiny and disgustingly cute." Her mom was five-one and so very dainty. The twins took after her. Walt was taller, but not by a whole lot.

"Bring 'em on." Travis entered the room and came toward her in long purposeful strides. When he reached the bed where she sat, he dropped down beside her. He laid his hand on her thigh.

It felt good there. Too good. She gave him a rueful glance and warned, "Your mom and Mercy and Elena and I are going shopping in half an hour."

His warm fingers stayed right where they were. "You shopped all day yesterday."

"That was Black Friday."

"So? Shopping is shopping."

"Spoken like a man."

He leaned close enough to nibble on her ear. "A man starved for his woman's undivided attention."

She picked up that tempting hand of his and put it down on *his* thigh. "I'm sorry. I have to go. Yesterday we bought mostly Christmas presents. Today we're doing wedding stuff. Mainly we'll be looking for my wedding dress. And we're visiting a florist and bakery to talk flowers and cake."

He put his hand back on her leg and bent close a second time to nuzzle her neck. "I can be fast when I need to be. This won't take long at all."

The warmth of his breath, the damp scent of his hair, still wet from the shower, the just-shaved feel of his cheek against hers...they all conspired to make her weaken. And yearn. She really couldn't get enough of him. "I still have to, um, call my dad..."

"Like I said. I'll make this quick." He went right to work, sliding his hand up into the cove of her thighs, cupping her over her jeans.

Sighing in surrender, she eased her thighs apart. "Not *too* quick."

He unzipped her zipper, undid the snap. "Quick, but not too quick. Coming right up."

"Oh, Travis..." She let him guide her back across the bed.

And for a little while, she forgot all about her mom and her stepdad and the Terrible Twins, about the wedding that was going to be upon them in a few too-short weeks. She forgot her fears and her doubts and her insecurities.

There was just the two of them, her and Travis, alone, making beautiful, perfect, just-right love.

Twenty minutes later, she called her dad.

Ted Jaworski's response was laughter. Sam's dad was six-foot-ten and barrel-chested. He had arms like tree trunks. And when he laughed it could make the floor shake. "Travis?" He sucked in a breath and laughed some more. "You're marryin' *Travis?*"

Sam gritted her teeth. "Yeah, Dad. And you and Keisha are invited."

"That rich boy take advantage of my little girl?"

Sam loved her dad, but he could really annoy her without half trying. "Travis is not a boy. And I am not the least bit little."

Ted gave another of those ground-shaking laughs. "You know what I told him when he first showed up and started sniffin' around you."

"Oh, come on, Dad. Travis is not some hound dog. He never *sniffed* around me. Never."

"Maybe you didn't think so. But a father notices that kind of thing—and anyway, you haven't let me tell you what I told him."

As if she wanted to know. "Dad—"

"I said, 'Travis Bravo, you lay a hand on my little girl and I'll take it off with a hacksaw.'" Ted laughed some more.

She waited for him to wind down a little before remarking, "You know, Dad, I could have gone my whole life without knowing that."

"I don't believe it. You and Travis. Gettin' hitched. What do you know?"

"That's right. Travis and I are getting married. The question is, are you and Keisha coming?"

"We wouldn't miss it, baby girl. It's out at that big Bravo spread down there in Texas, right?"

"That's right."

"Lots of open land. And in Texas, they don't have all that many stupid laws against fireworks...."

"Dad. Listen. I mean it. No."

"Did I ask you a question? I don't think I asked you any question."

"No fireworks, Dad. Do you hear me?"

If he did hear, he refused to admit it. "We're comin'," he announced. "With bells on. You count on it, baby. I'll be there to give my little girl away."

* * *

Sam found her dress that day. It was snow-white satin, with a halter top that bared most of her back. She also chose the flowers she wanted in her bouquet, in blue and purple, with touches of white. She and Aleta agreed her colors were purple and blue, with silver and white for accents.

"Perfect for a holiday wedding," Aleta declared.

Sam's head was spinning by the time they got to the bakery. There were as many options when it came to a cake as there were for wedding dresses and bridal bouquets. She met with the bakery's wedding consultant and couldn't decide.

Which was fine, as it turned out, because Travis was supposed to get input on the cake. The cake lady suggested that Sam and her groom return to the bakery on Monday and make their choice.

Monday. The make-believe week of playing Travis's bride was supposed to be over Sunday. Travis had planned to return to Houston. Sam had a plane ticket for San Diego.

But then make-believe had somehow become reality.

She turned numbly to Aleta, who sat beside her. "We're supposed to leave Sunday...."

Aleta gave her a fond smile. "It's all workable, don't worry." She told the cake lady, "We'll call you early in the week and get everything settled."

"It's simple," Travis said that night when they were alone in their rooms. "I'll stay an extra day. I'll go to Houston on Tuesday. Worst case, I'll need up to a couple of weeks to wrap things up with STOI."

They were sitting on the bed together. She dropped

back across the mattress, face up. "So you're doing it? Going to work for BravoCorp?"

He stretched out on his side next to her. "Yeah. Is that okay with you?"

"Of course." She stared past him, at the milk-glass ceiling fixture mounted on a plaster medallion above. "If it's what you really want."

"It is." He sounded absolutely certain.

She could use a little more of that, of certainty—not about Travis. She had no doubt that he was the one for her. But about everything else, she wasn't so sure. All day, as she shopped for her wedding dress and chose her bouquet and listened to the cake lady go on about ganache and fondant and raspberry fillings, she'd felt kind of wispy and fragile, two words she'd never before even considered in connection with herself. She asked in a voice that sounded distant to her own ears, "So we'll be looking for a house in San Antonio?"

He touched her shoulder. "Sam, are you okay?"

She turned her head toward him, gave him a smile that only wobbled a little. "So much is happening. I'm a little dazed, I guess. I've still got my ticket to San Diego for Sunday."

Sunday, when it was all supposed to have been over. When her sweet fantasy of loving Travis—of having him want to spend his life with her—would be only a memory. When her magic carriage turned into a pumpkin and her ball gown into rags.

Except now, it wasn't going to be over. Now, she really was Travis's true love.

And they were getting married in two and a half weeks.

"Cancel it," he said.

She blinked, refocused on his dear face. The plane

ticket. They were talking about her flight to California. "Guess I'll have to." She folded her hands on her stomach.

He rested his hand on hers. "You can stay here for as long as you and Mom need to do all the wedding stuff. Then you can fly to Houston, stay with me at the town house. We should be back here by a week before the wedding, I'm hoping. As soon as we get here, we can start looking for a house."

She thought of her place in San Diego, her own private retreat from the world. Would he ask her to give that up? He just might. She had to be ready for that.

The wispy, fragile feelings faded. She was instantly stronger, more like her old self.

No. Not a chance.

She wouldn't give up her San Diego apartment. No way. "I want to keep my condo in San Diego."

He bent close, kissed her. "No problem." He said it easily, without the least hesitation.

Well, good. That wouldn't be an issue, then. And the more she thought about San Diego, the more she wished she could steal a little time there—to get her bearings. To decompress. "In fact, maybe I'll fly to California while you're in Houston. I can spend a couple of days packing up the things I want to bring with me to our new house here." Yeah, it was a great idea. She could catch her breath there for a day or two, get a break from the big rush to the altar.

His eyes held hers.

And she knew then. Absolutely.

He was going to try to stop her from going to her place. And she wasn't allowing that. She couldn't allow that.

And that meant they were going to end up arguing.

He said, "Every night you're not in my bed is one night too many away from you."

Oh, yeah. She knew what he would say next. He was going to tell her that he wanted her to come straight to Houston, that he wanted her with him, not off on the beach in California.

Sam braced herself to make a stand.

Chapter Twelve

And then Travis said, "But sure. Fly to San Diego. Pack up what you want to bring. Ship it here and store it, or have it shipped once we get our house."

She gulped. She couldn't believe it. She'd been ready for a fight. And there wasn't going to be one—not about this anyway. "Uh. Sure. All right. I'll do that."

His eyes were gleaming. He seemed so happy, making plans—for their future. "And I thought we could save the honeymoon until after the holidays. Then maybe we'll go someplace in January or February, someplace tropical, with blue lagoons and palm trees...."

That did sound kind of nice. But where was the catch?

Wait a minute.

Maybe there was no catch. Maybe she ought to stop looking for problems where there really weren't any.

"I would like that," she said, meaning it. And then, well, why hold back? They needed to revisit the issue of her career plans. Now was as good a time as any. "I'm thinking I can take online courses over the winter. And in the spring, I'll see about getting into the college of business at UT San Antonio for the fall semester."

He bent close again. "Still determined to get that degree and become an accountant, huh?"

She looked at him levelly, though her heart had kicked into overdrive as her adrenaline was suddenly surging. "Yes, I am. Any objections?"

"Hell, no. You've got a dream and you have a right to make it real."

She tried not to stare openmouthed as the surge faded off, leaving her feeling slightly hollow and more than a little ashamed of jumping to yet another conclusion.

She reached up, touched his beloved face, dared to ask, "What about how I need to get pregnant and stay home where you can protect me?"

He gave her a wry grin. "Well, I thought about that. And I decided you were right. About all of it. I hate that I can't protect you from anything that might ever happen to you. But that's how it is. What I *can* do is everything in my power to see that you're happy. I want you to have what you want—everything you want."

She searched his face, hardly able to believe that he had come so far on this big issue—so far and so fast. She should probably quit while she was ahead. But then she heard herself asking, "And a baby…?"

He kissed her nose. "I rethought that a little, too. I was thinking, if we could start trying in, say, a year? That would give us some time just for us."

"Oh, Travis…" She wrapped her hand around the

back of his neck and brought him closer to her. "A year would be workable. I could go for a year."

He looked pretty pleased with himself. "See? I can take a hint."

"You can. And you did. You amaze me sometimes."

"Good. A man needs to be amazing. At least now and then."

She laughed and then she kissed him. And then she whispered, "Time for us. We need that."

"Yeah, we do." He kissed her cheek, her nose again, the other cheek.

She bit her lower lip, as the enormity of it all flooded over her again. "And even given that we're waiting a year before we start trying, well…a baby. And a college degree. And a new career. It's a lot."

"I would help." He kissed the space between her brows. "And with me working for BravoCorp, the money will be no issue. We can hire quality childcare to give you a break, and someone dependable to cook and clean."

"When you put it like that, it all seems possible."

"It *is* possible, Sam. With you and me, together, there's nothing we can't do."

Monday, as planned, they went to the bakery and chose a dark chocolate cake with chocolate ganache and mocha buttercream filling. The icing would be white buttercream with pearled borders. Real orchids, purple ones, would cover the top layer and cascade down over the two lower tiers.

Tuesday morning early, she drove him to the airport and he caught a flight to Houston. He left his Cadillac for her to use.

Travis called that night. They talked for hours. And

when they finally said goodbye, the silence that followed left her yearning and empty and longing to call him all over again, just to hear his voice.

That made her feel weak and needy, which were two things Sam Jaworski was not and had never been. Until now.

He wasn't all that far away and they'd be back together soon.

Still, she missed him. So much.

It was scary, really. To feel that way. To ache all over just for a certain man's tender touch. For the sound of his voice, the brush of his lips against hers.

She'd spent a lot of her life wishing she might feel just this way. And now that she did, well, it was magic.

And it was awful, too. Fearsome and huge and more than she'd bargained for.

She slept in the bed in the blue room where they'd spent most of their nights during Thanksgiving week. It made her feel closer to him.

He called Wednesday night, too. He said it looked like he would be back in San Antonio by the middle of the following week. STOI was sorry to see him go. They'd even offered a nice promotion and a generous raise and benefits package if he would stay on. He'd thanked them and turned them down. And since the *Deepwater Venture* project had wrapped up, he was at an ending point anyway. It wasn't all that complicated to wind things down.

He asked how all the wedding preparations were going.

Sam laughed. "Your mother's a marvel."

"So I'm guessing that means it's going well?"

"Better than well. There's really nothing for me to do."

A silence on the line, then, "You okay with that?"

She laughed. "Are you kidding? I'm thrilled with that."

"Well, if you feel like she's taking over…"

"No way. Your mom's not like that."

He grunted, a disbelieving sound. "Come on, she does have a bossy side. You know she does."

"Not with me. With me, she's…" Her throat locked up and her eyes got misty. Sheesh. She was getting to be a frickin' emotional disaster lately, she truly was.

"Sam? Still there?"

She made herself answer around the lump in her throat. "Right here."

"You all right? You seem kind of—"

"I'm great." She said it with feeling—maybe more feeling than necessary. "And I love your mom. She's the best. Don't you say a word against her or you'll be answering to me."

"Whoa. Next you'll be saying how you can take me."

"Yeah, well." She put on her best macho bluster. "You know I can."

He chuckled then. It was a very sexy sound. "Anytime. I'll be looking forward to it."

"You're so easy."

"Only for you."

She suggested, "And listen, on the night before the wedding?"

"What about it?"

Her cheeks felt too warm. She knew she was blushing, which was silly. "I was thinking we could sleep in separate rooms. You know, be a little bit traditional. Is that dumb, do you think?"

"However you want it, Sam. That's how it'll be."

"Well, I want that, for you not to see me on our wedding day until I walk down the aisle to you. I don't know why I want it exactly. But I do."

"You got it."

They talked some more, about the wedding, about the house they would be looking for, about how soon they would be together again.

After she hung up, she had that too-familiar burning need. To call him back. To hear his voice…

Really. What she *needed* was to get a grip.

Her mom called on Thursday. Yes, she and Walt and the twins would *love* to stay at the ranch for the wedding. "We don't mind roughing it a bit for your big day."

Sam laughed. "Well, don't worry, Mom. You won't have to rough it at all. The ranch house is more of a mansion really. It's surrounded by beautiful gardens. There's a big pool with a fountain and wading pool and spa. And there are tennis courts…"

"Oh. Well." Her mom sounded stunned. "All right, then. It sounds very nice. We'll arrive on Friday morning, stay over for the wedding Saturday afternoon. And return home Sunday afternoon."

"I'll tell Mercy. She'll be pleased."

"And honestly. I should do *something*, Samantha. I want to help out. After all, I *am* the mother of the bride."

"Mom. It's fine. You don't have to. It's a very small wedding and Aleta—Travis's mom—she's taking care of everything."

There was a silence, followed by a small, pitiful sniffling sound.

Oh, no. "Mom? Mom, are you crying?"

Her mother sobbed outright. "I never thought you would get married. Not to a man anyway. I never even thought you *liked* men…."

Terrific. A sexual orientation talk with the mother

she hardly knew. Not. Going. To. Happen. "Mom. Come on, Mom, don't cry…"

"I'm sorry. I'm so sorry…" There was more sobbing. The sobs had that scary sound. The sound that said she was never going to stop.

"Mom. Hey. It's okay. There's nothing to be sorry about."

"We never did get along. I never…understood you." Her mother hiccupped and then sobbed again. "Hold on, I need a tissue…."

"Mom. Really. We don't need to…" She heard a delicate, distant honking sound. Her mother blowing her nose.

And then she was back on the line again. "You're so…big, Samantha." A tight sob. Another honk at the tissue. "You're just like your father. Big and strong and loud and overbearing. You always make me feel so small. So…insignificant."

"Uh, well. Gee, thanks."

Her mother let out a small, sad little wail. "Oh, now I've gone and put my foot in it. Now you'll hate me even more than ever."

"Mom, I don't hate you."

"You do. You know you do. You always did. Your father turned you against me on the day you were born…."

"Mom, come on. Don't go there. Please?"

Her mom went right on as though Sam hadn't spoken. "And we never bonded and now you're getting married and you don't want me to be involved in any part of it."

"Mom, hold on. I invited you, didn't I?"

"I'm sure you felt you had to."

Okay. Too true for comfort. "Look, um…" Good frickin' gravy. What to say next? "You really want to be involved?"

"Oh, didn't I just *say* that? See, that's another thing. You never listen to me when I speak. Just like your—"

"Mom, I'm going to hook you up with Aleta, okay?"

"A-Aleta?" Sniffle. Honk. "Your fiancé's mother?"

Please don't hate me for this, Aleta. "Yeah, Travis's mom. She will call you. Today. She'll…get with you."

"G-get with me?"

"Yeah, you know, consult with you. Get your input and assistance on what has to be done. I know she'll be so happy to have help." *Oh, I am a stone liar and I am going straight to hell.*

"She will?"

"Of course." Like there was anything left to do. Like there was anything her mom could do anyway up there in Minneapolis. "And to…get to know you. She's real big on family, Aleta is."

"She is?"

"Yeah. Real big." Well, at least that part was true. "Are you going to be home for a while?"

"I…well, yes. I'm at home. The twins are at school. Walt is at the office. I'm just thinking of what to put together for dinner."

"All right. I'll have Aleta call you."

"But when?"

"Right away."

"In a few minutes?"

"Aleta's not here right now. But as soon as I see her and give her your number. Within the next couple of hours."

"Oh, Samantha. I don't want to butt in."

Oh, yes, you do. "It's fine, Mom. It's good. She'll call. Within the hour."

"All—all right. All right, Samantha. I…well, I love you, you know?"

"I love you, too, Mom," Sam said because that's what you say when your mom says she loves you. And then, finally, she managed to say goodbye.

The minute she hung up, she knew she should call her mom right back and bust to the truth that Aleta didn't need anyone's help, that everything was pretty much done and her mom should just come to the wedding and leave it at that.

But if she called her mom back, there would be more crying.

Sam couldn't stand that. She felt like crying herself half the time lately. She just might crack if she had to listen to one more of her mother's sad little sobs.

Yeah, it was wrong to drag Aleta into this. But then again, if anyone could make the situation better, it would be Aleta.

Unfortunately, Aleta and Davis had gone back to their own house in a ritzy San Antonio neighborhood the day before. It was bad enough to ask this of Travis's mom. She couldn't do it over the phone.

She called Aleta, but only to make sure she was home.

Travis's mom answered on the first ring. Sam wanted to burst into tears then, just at the warm sound of Aleta's voice.

She held it together. "Hey, it's Sam. I was wondering if I could come by now for a few minutes?"

Aleta said, "Of course."

A half an hour later, Sam was sitting next to Travis's mom on a sofa in the sun room of Aleta's beautiful Olmos Park house, a delicate china cup filled with coffee in her hands and a plate of sugared pecan cookies on the low table in front of them.

Sam groaned. "I don't even know how to ask you this."

Aleta sipped from her china cup. "Anything. I hope you know that."

Sam set her cup and saucer down before she dropped them. She wanted to lean on Travis's mom, just put her head on the smaller woman's slender shoulder. "I've done a bad, bad thing."

Aleta set her cup and saucer next to Sam's. And then she did exactly what Sam had longed for her to do. She put an arm around Sam and drew her closer. "Tell me. We'll fix it. Together."

Sam let her shoulders slump. "It's my mother. There's no fixing my mother...."

"Oh, no. She's not able to come to the wedding after all?"

"No, it's not that. She's coming. But she's hurt because I didn't include her in the planning part. She wants to help. And I...I'm so sorry, Aleta. I didn't know what to do, so I told her you might have something she could do and I would have you call her."

Aleta smiled. A *real* smile. "Perfect."

Sam hung her head and made a low sound of pure misery. "You say that now, but wait until you talk to her. She will drive you insane. And it's not like you even need her help."

"But, honey, *she* needs to help, to be involved. You can see that, can't you?"

Sam grunted. Even if it was unfeminine. "Yeah, I suppose so."

"And it's great. Because this way she and I will get to know each other a little. And she'll be a part of the wedding. And she'll feel better about everything."

"You make it sound so...simple and clear."

"But it's not—not to you, and probably not to your mom. I understand that. My mother is gone now. But she and I...we had our issues, believe me. It's the first love, between a mother and her child. Sometimes it's a very painful love."

"Oh, Aleta. She said that I hate her. I *don't.*"

"I know. You told me. That first day you and Travis arrived at the ranch, remember?"

"I just... I never really thought that she even cared. But I guess she did."

Aleta touched Sam's hair, a light, fond touch—there and then gone. "That's important. For you to know that."

"So why doesn't it make me feel any better? I just feel...confused." And about a lot more than just her mother, if the truth were told.

"Big changes are stressful. Even good changes. It will be fine. You'll see."

Sam took Aleta's soft, beautifully manicured hand. "Thank you. Thank you from the bottom of my heart."

"You are more than welcome. And you are not to worry. Your mom and I will get together and talk and she'll choose the things she wants to do. Maybe the dinner menu—or any of the wedding weekend meals. There will be several. We haven't firmed those up yet. What does she enjoy doing?"

"Um, knitting. Sewing. Scrapbooking. Baking. She loves to make those novelty cakes. Cakes shaped like guitars, a bunch of cupcakes arranged to look like a bear or a giraffe or a giant flower...." She'd made Sam an oil derrick birthday cake once, with chocolate syrup for crude oil. That had been the weekend when the twins snickered every time she got near them.

Aleta squeezed her shoulder. "See? There are lots of possibilities for her to choose from. This is wonderful."

"Oh, Aleta. You say that now…."

"I say it because it's true. She loves you and she wants to help and that's what matters."

"You're right. You're absolutely right."

Aleta picked up the plate of cookies. "Now have a cookie and let me have your mother's number. I'll give her a call."

Aleta really was a wonder. She got Sam's mom working on some special surprise. Evidently, her mom was pleased with whatever it was she had in the works. She called Sam later that night and said what a sweet woman Aleta was and how she and Walt and the twins were really looking forward to their Texas visit, to meeting Travis and his family and being there for Samantha's special day.

Disaster averted, thanks to Aleta.

Friday, Aleta came out to the ranch and they discussed the wedding dinner.

After two hours of talking about menus and place cards and centerpieces, Sam crossed her eyes and pretended to fall against the couch cushions in a dead faint. "Any more wedding talk and I swear it will be the end of me."

Aleta laughed. "Well, that's fine because we're good to go. I have what I need from you and you don't have to hear the word *wedding* for at least the next week."

"Hah. Can I get that in writing?"

Aleta sent her sly glance. "Well, there may be an occasional *mention* of flowers or table arrangements…"

"See? I knew you didn't really mean it." Sam sat up straight. "But if we are pretty much on top of things, I was planning to take a few days at my place in San Diego before I meet Travis in Houston…."

"Well, then, go."

"You're sure?"

"I'm adamant. Go."

The next morning, Sam flew to San Diego International.

She was at her beach condo by noon—well, okay, her *near*-the-beach condo. From her living room window, if she squinted, it was just possible to see a tiny slice of the blue Pacific between a pair of luxury high-rises.

The beach wasn't far away, however. She could get there on foot from her front door. That afternoon she walked barefoot along the shore for over two hours. Then she went back to the condo and started packing. Travis called at seven. They talked until ten.

The next day, she walked for three hours and had the rest of her packing done by dark. She poured a glass of wine and went out onto her tiny balcony—and wished she was in Houston, with Travis at the town house.

She'd had some vague idea that being at her place, on her own, by the beach, would clear away the wispy, wimpy feelings, make her more like herself again.

But it didn't. Not really. Being alone only made her ache all the harder for Travis, made her feel itchy and uncomfortable in her own skin.

When he called an hour later, she told him she would be there, with him, the next day.

He met her at the airport, by the baggage carousel. She ran to his arms and kissed him until she felt like her lips might fall off. It was a serious get-a-room kiss. And when they finally stepped apart, both gasping for air, he grabbed her suitcase in one hand and her arm in the other and hustled her out to where he had a limo waiting.

They went straight to his place, where they fell into bed together and didn't get up until dinnertime.

The next day was Tuesday. He went off for his last day at STOI. His town house was stacked with boxes. He'd been working hard, getting himself packed for the move to San Antonio.

She spent the day filling more boxes with his things. And she spent the night in his arms.

They flew back to San Antonio the next day and headed for the ranch, where they would be staying until they got their own place. Thursday, they started looking for a house—which they found on Friday. They made an offer that afternoon.

By Monday, after a couple of counteroffers, they signed the contract. They would be moving in the first week in January.

When they left the Realtor's office, Travis kissed her and headed off to BravoCorp for his first day in the family business. Sam watched him walk away from her and wished she had a job to go to.

She went back to the ranch and got on the internet and signed up for three online accounting classes that would start in the second week of January. That should keep her busy—or it would when January finally rolled around.

Getting that edgy-under-the-skin feeling, she wrapped the presents she'd bought on Black Friday. Once the wrapping was done, she carried all the ones for the Bravos down to put under the giant tree that Mercy and Aleta had put up in the living room. On one of the lower branches, she also hung the Betty Boop ornament she'd bought that day in Fredericksburg.

Mercy gave her some priority-mail boxes and she put the presents that had to be mailed in those, and addressed them. Most were for her mom and her mom's family. There was also one for Ted and one for Keisha. She sent that to the P.O. box they kept in Tucson. And finally, there were the suspenders for Jonathan. She slipped a note in the box, inviting him to the wedding.

No, she didn't really expect him to come. But still. It seemed only right that he should be there if he could make it.

Mercy, a large animal vet, was going through nearby Kerrville on her way to treat some farmer's sick goat. She took Sam's packages to mail.

After Mercy left, Sam put on jeans and some old work boots she'd brought back from her condo and went out to the stables. Once she convinced Luke that she really wanted to pitch in, he put her to work mucking out stalls. Just like old times, back on the ranch in South Dakota. She broke a nail in the process.

Jonathan would not have approved.

For the rest of the week, she spent a few hours in the stables every day. Luke seemed happy to have her help and she got along with the hands just fine. It was better—*she* was better—when she kept busy.

That last week before the wedding, which seemed to drag by in some respects, was gone in an instant.

Her dad and Keisha arrived Thursday evening. They rolled up in the Winnebago at a little before dinnertime. She'd been watching for them and ran out to greet them.

Her dad emerged, wearing Wranglers, rawhide boots, a straw cowboy hat and a plaid Western shirt, his belly hanging over his belt buckle, his laugh booming out. "There's my baby girl…"

"Dad!" She ran to him. Still laughing, he enfolded her in his beefy arms. He smelled of the cheap cigarettes he wouldn't stop smoking and his laughter seemed to shake the world.

When he stopped squeezing the breath out of her, he took her arms and held her away from him. "Will you look at you?" He let out a long, piercing wolf whistle. "Hotter'n a firecracker. It's a whole new Sam."

She smiled up at him. "Dad, glad you could make it."

Travis was right behind her. "Ted, how you been?"

Her dad reached for Travis's hand. "Been messin' with my baby, have you? Didn't I warn you about that?"

Travis laughed. He'd always liked her dad and had never been the least put off by the loud laugh and booming voice—let alone the towering size. "What can I say? Guilty. And really, really happy about it."

"Well, as long as you're marryin' her, I guess I'll have to let you live."

Sam caught sight of Keisha then. Her dad's girlfriend was just stepping down from the motor home. As usual, she had her red hair in tight cornrows. She wore a long, baggy dress with a bulky gray sweater that looked like she'd stolen it from some absentminded professor, suede elbow patches and all.

Keisha smiled wide, showing the cute gap between her two front teeth. "Sam! Hey! Wow! Look at you! You are lookin' *good!*" Somehow, everything Keisha said sounded like it had an exclamation point after it. She was the most enthusiastic person Sam had ever known.

"Hey, Keisha. Thanks. It's good to see you." Even with the baggy dress and sweater, Sam could see that Keisha's belly was bigger than Ted's. She went and gave Keisha a hug, felt the bulge of the younger woman's stomach pressing into hers.

Yep. Definitely. Her dad's girlfriend was pregnant.

Her dad was laughing again. "Surprise! You're getting a little brother or sister, baby girl. Me and Keisha are expecting the first week in March."

"I *know* he's brought fireworks," Sam said between clenched teeth later that night, when she and Travis were alone.

Travis sat next to her on the bed checking his investments on his laptop. "You know your dad. One of a kind."

She elbowed him in the ribs. Hard. "When he sets them off in the middle of the night and then burns down the stables sneaking a smoke, you won't be so thrilled with his rugged individualism—and what was he thinking? He's almost sixty. He smokes too much. They live in a frickin' motor home. And, true, Keisha's about the nicest, happiest person on the planet, but she's never seemed much like the motherly type."

"She's a good woman. She'll manage. And maybe they're planning on settling down."

"Yeah. Right. When porcupines get Visa cards."

Travis laughed and put his laptop on the night table. Then he hauled her close and kissed her until she almost forgot that her dad and his girlfriend would soon be giving her another half sibling young enough to be her own child.

When he lifted his mouth from hers, she gained several IQ points and remembered all the things that were bothering her. "And tomorrow, my mother and *her* family are coming."

He took both her wrists and pinned them to the bed beside her head. "It's terrific that they're coming."

"The twins will be following me from room to room, snickering behind their hands."

"No, they won't."

"Yes, they will. Secretly, they've always believed I was really a man."

"But I'll be there. To attest to your womanhood with a wide, happy and very satisfied grin on my face."

"Don't you dare."

"Sam. Relax, will you? You're way too tense about everything."

"I am. It's true. I'm a nervous wreck. Me. Sam Jaworski. Who could arm wrestle half the roughnecks on the *Deepwater Venture* and win two out of three. What's happening to me?"

He bent close, nipped her earlobe. "You're getting married."

"Yeah. Whoever thought *that* would happen? Not my family, that's for sure."

He grazed her chin with his teeth. "Let me take your mind off your problems...." He kissed her breast right through her silk shirt and lacy bra.

She moaned and tried to pull free of his grip. "Let go of my wrists, will you?"

"Not until you promise you won't say another word all night about your dad or your mom or anyone in your family." He kissed her other breast.

For a long time.

Finally, sighing, she whispered, "My family? What family?"

"That's the spirit."

But he still didn't let go of her wrists. Not for several minutes. Not until she was enthusiastically begging him for more.

The Carlsons arrived at ten-thirty the next morning.

At her first sight of the new Sam, Dina said, "Huh? Puh-lease. No way."

Mila didn't say anything that Sam could hear. But she did whisper something behind her hand.

Their mother burst into tears. "Oh, Samantha. You're beautiful. Oh, Samantha. I never knew…."

Walt, looking slightly befuddled as always behind the heavy black frames of his glasses, said, "Ahem, well. Samantha. What a nice surprise." Sam wasn't sure if he meant the changes in her—or that she'd finally found someone willing to marry her.

Sam introduced them to Travis. He said how happy he was to meet them at last. He actually seemed to mean it. He shook Walt's hand, kissed her mother on the cheek and gave each of the Terrible Twins a warm and welcoming smile. Really, he was a prince in the truest sense of the word.

Her mother, so tiny and delicate in a pink suit and ruffled lilac-colored blouse, stared up at him, wet-eyed. "Well, I am so pleased to meet you, too, Travis. I can't tell you *how* pleased…"

Paco and one of the other hands were there, ready to help.

Travis said, "Paco and Bobby will take your bags inside."

"Oh!" Her mother gave him a trembling smile of over-the-top gratitude. "Thank you so much, Travis. Yes."

And then Ted appeared, smoking a cigarette, bearing down on them from the driveway that led to the garage and the space beside it where he had parked the Winnebago. Keisha waddled along in his wake.

Sam's mother watched them approach, a look of absolute horror on her fine-boned face. "I see your father has already arrived," she said weakly. "And he still hasn't stopped smoking." Was she going to faint, right there in the driveway? She'd damn well better not.

"That's right," Travis said cheerfully, as if everyone's mother got the vapors like some anemic heroine from a Victorian novel—as if everyone's dad had a pregnant girlfriend less than half his age. "He and Keisha got here yesterday."

"Ah. Yes," Jennifer said feebly. "Keisha. Of course."

The twins snickered and whispered to each other as their mother kind of sagged against Walt, who put his arm around her and pushed his glasses back up the bridge of his nose.

Ted descended on them. He dropped his cigarette and stomped it with his big boot. "Well, if it isn't Jennifer and Walt and their two gorgeous girls."

Keisha was right behind him, her hand under her belly to stop it from bouncing as she hurried to keep up with Ted's giant strides. "Hello! I'm Keisha! So amazing to meet you at last!"

Inside, Sam introduced her mom and Walt and the twins to Aleta and Davis.

Travis's parents were great. They shook hands and smiled sincerely and said all the right things. Then Sam led the Carlsons up to their rooms.

The twins went straight into their room and shut the door. Which was fine with Sam. Great, actually.

She wasn't so lucky when it came to her mom.

Jennifer wanted to talk. She shooed Walt from the room and took Sam's big hand in her tiny little pink one. "Samantha, sit with me." There were a pair of ladder-back chairs by the window. Her mom led her over there and they sat. Sam couldn't help recalling how Aleta had done more or less the same thing, that first day Sam arrived at the ranch with Travis. But somehow, when Aleta did it, Sam had felt flattered and only too happy to chat. With her mom, she dreaded what might happen next. "Now," said Jennifer. "Tell me everything."

Everything. Right. "Gee, Mom. That would take a while."

It was, of course, totally the wrong thing to say. Her mom's pretty face crumpled and her eyes filled with tears. "I only…I just thought we might…touch base a little. Is that so much to ask?"

It wasn't. Sam knew it wasn't. "Of course not. What did you want to know?"

Her mother pressed her lips together, put on a smile and tried again. "Well, I mean, look at you. You're *gorgeous*."

"Thanks, Mom."

"How…well, I always knew you had good bones. That you could be attractive if you'd only try. And now you're…I have no words. I'm just stunned."

"It's a long story."

"And I would love to hear every detail."

Sam had to admit that her mom was being kind of sweet really. That she was only trying to be appreciative and supportive. So Sam gave her an abridged version of the makeover, leaving out the part about how it had all started because Travis needed a fake fiancée. Sam said that she had wanted to make a change and getting professional help seemed like the best way.

When she was done, her mom clapped her little hands. "Oh, that is wonderful, Samantha. I'm so proud of you." Jennifer. Proud of her. That was a first.

Sam basked in the moment. "Well, thanks, Mom."

"And let me guess the rest. Your old friend Travis

took one look at the new you and realized how blind he'd been."

"Pretty much, yeah."

"And now, here you are, getting married to your own personal prince charming."

That made her smile. "He is a prince, isn't he?"

"I know you must be so happy at last, to be in love with a wonderful man and to know that he loves you back."

"I am happy. Very much so." *Not that I wasn't before.*

"And if you had only listened to me, this could have happened years ago."

Bam. The sucker punch. As always. Sam kept her cool, even though her stomach had tied itself in about a hundred little knots. "Well, I didn't listen to you. And it didn't happen until now. And I'm more than happy with the way things have turned out."

Her mother shook her pretty blond head. "Oh, Samantha. Always so proud."

"I'm only saying that it all worked out. Can we leave it at that?"

"Of course," said her mother. She meant, *of course not.* "I just…well, I don't have to tell you. I mean, what can your father be *thinking?*"

It was pretty much what Sam had said to Travis the night before. But somehow, when her mom said it, it sounded snotty and mean-spirited. "Leave it alone, Mom."

"Yes, well. I suppose I should."

"Please."

"It's a terrible embarrassment. In front of Travis's lovely family."

"The Bravos don't seem to mind. They seem to think

Dad's kind of fun. And everybody likes Keisha. I mean, what's not to like?"

"But is he going to *marry* her?"

Sam realized that on top of her stomach hurting, she was getting a headache. "I don't know, Mom. I figure that's none of my business."

Her mother visibly flinched. "What was that? One of those barely veiled criticisms of yours?"

You ought to know, Mom, Sam thought but somehow managed not to say. Barely veiled criticisms were her mother's weapon of choice. Sam got up. "I don't want to fight with you, Mom. I just don't."

Her mother rose, too. "You're right," she said stiffly. "I don't want to fight either. I only want for us to get along."

The day before the wedding continued. Endlessly.

There was lunch in the sun room, where her mother and father actively ignored each other—her father talking too loud and too much, her mother saying little, but making small, outraged, impatient sounds and constantly pinching up her small pink lips. The twins, their sleek blond heads pressed close together, snickered constantly. Walt looked befuddled and Keisha occasionally said something harmless and sweet with the usual exclamation point after it.

The Bravos—Davis and Aleta, Mercy and Luke and Travis, too—took it all in stride. Sam knew they weren't bothered in the least by her dysfunctional family. They made easy conversation and filled in the hostile silences with new, interesting and yet uncontroversial topics of discussion. Little Lucas was his usual adorable self and baby Serena lived up to her name, sitting quietly with her toys around her, beaming up at anyone who stopped and spoke to her.

Sam's headache got worse. She wondered how she had gotten here, in this big, beautiful house, with Travis's wonderful family and her totally messed up one. She thought of the *Deepwater Venture*—of all the rigs she'd worked on. And she saw herself, tall and capable and spattered with grease and drilling mud, striding confidently across the drilling platform, secure in her idea of herself and her place in the world.

She didn't feel so secure now. She felt like she didn't have a clue who she really was. She had no idea where she was going.

Or if she would ever get there.

Did other brides feel this way? For all their sakes—and the sake of their poor grooms—she hoped not.

The other Bravos started arriving around four. Dinner that night was sort of a rehearsal dinner, just minus the rehearsal.

They all came, each of Travis's brothers and sisters, and their wives and husbands and kids, too. Dinner went nicely, Sam thought. With so many people there, her hulking, loud dad and passive-aggressive mom kind of disappeared in the crowd. She started to believe she just might make it through the weekend after all.

After dinner, Travis's brothers kidnapped him. All the men—Walt and Sam's dad included—drove away in various vehicles to meet up at some agreed-upon location for an impromptu bachelor party.

Sam and the other women stood on the porch, laughing and waving, as the men drove away.

When he came back, Travis would sleep alone in the blue room that night. And Sam would stay in the yellow room, with the door shut between them. She'd really wanted it that way when she asked him if they could sleep separately on the last night before the wedding.

But somehow, as the evening went on and Sam visited with her soon-to-be sisters-in-law and Aleta and Keisha, and tried to be nice to her mom and the Terrible Twins, she found herself wishing that when he came home, he would go straight to the door between their rooms, push it open and climb into bed with her. There was something about his solid presence in the bed that eased her fears and calmed her anxieties.

With Travis's strong arms around her, she knew who she was again. Her doubts about whether she was cut out to be his wife—to be *anyone's* wife—seemed meaningless and easy to ignore.

It was midnight when she climbed the stairs to the yellow room. She shut the door to the hall and also the one to the blue room. Then she stood at the windows for a long time and stared at the new sliver of moon out there in the wide Texas sky and wondered what was wrong with her.

She didn't like her mother much and she wanted to bitch-slap both of her half sisters. Her dad drove her nuts.

But her birth family wasn't what this weekend was about. This weekend was about her and Travis. Travis, whom she loved.

Travis, who was just right for her, who made her body glow with pleasure and who warmed her once-lonely heart.

She was the luckiest woman in the world.

So why was she longing to run away from her own wedding?

Chapter Thirteen

Travis accepted another Jack Black on the rocks and joined in the drinking song Ted had started.

As bachelor parties went, it was a tame one, held in one of the wood-paneled rooms at his father's club. Tame was fine with Travis. There was some loud music—when Ted wasn't calling for it to be shut off so he could lead them in another raunchy song. The liquor flowed freely and there were even some good-looking women there. Not that any of his brothers, his brothers-in-law or his father seemed to care. A couple of his brothers had been players back in the day. But now, they were all like him. One-woman men.

Even Ted, who sure knew the lyrics to a lot of dirty ditties, wasn't the least interested in the bachelor party babes. True-blue to Keisha, who certainly deserved a good man. Walt, too, apparently, had no interest in a little bachelor party fooling around. He stayed well away from the women. Because he was too shy to try anything or because Jennifer was the only woman for him, Travis couldn't have said.

It was kind of fun really. Kicking back with the other men of the family, drinking a little more than he probably should have, listening to rock and roll and Christmas music and singing along with Ted.

Or it would have been fun, if Travis could only shake the scary feeling that he was going to lose Sam. The same as he'd lost Rachel. The same as he'd driven Wanda away.

Every night the past week or so, he would wake up at three or four in the morning and just lie there, watching Sam sleeping, thinking how he'd never felt the way he felt for her—not even with Rachel—and wondering what tricks God and fate and blind misfortune might have up their sleeves for him this time.

Yeah. All right. He had a problem. And he knew it. And he was working with it. He knew he had…issues, as a woman would put it. As Sam herself had put it a few weeks ago.

He knew that Sam was right when she said it wasn't his fault that Rachel had been run down by some out-of-it drunk driver. Sam was right when she said that he couldn't protect her from every single bad thing that might ever happen to her.

And as soon as he'd given some serious thought to those things that Sam had said, he'd taken steps to get past his own irrational terror of losing her.

He'd made himself back off on all the plans he had that hemmed her in. He'd agreed to put off trying to have a baby. He'd made it clear to her that he would support her in getting her degree and her start in accounting. He saw that it was only right, for her to have the life she wanted.

He *wanted* her to have the life she wanted.

Everything seemed good between them. Everything seemed right.

Except that sometimes, when he looked in her unforgettable blue eyes, he saw panic.

Sometimes he was sure he was losing her, even though he'd done everything he could think of to keep from driving her away.

He wanted the damn party to be over. He wanted to go back to the ranch and to Sam. Yeah, all right. They'd agreed to spend the night before their wedding in separate rooms.

Too bad about that. He wanted to shove open the door that separated them—to break it down, if he had to. He wanted to take her in his arms and never let her go. He wanted to tell her that she was everything to him and it was going to be all right.

But the bachelor party wasn't over. And he was the groom, so he had an obligation stay to the end.

Plus, well, what if his fears were all in his own mind?

Hey, it was possible. Because he had issues, deep-seated fears. And if the whole point was not to hem her in or freak her out, well, what could she feel but hemmed in and freaked out if he burst in on her in the middle of the night just to make sure she wasn't planning on running away from their wedding?

At some point, he had trust in her. Trust in what they had together. A man couldn't make a woman stay with him.

He could only be the best man he could be for her.

And let fate and God and blind misfortune do what they would.

Ted started another song. Travis raised his glass and joined in.

The party lasted until after three. Then he rode back to the ranch with his dad, Luke, Ted and Walt—Rogan went with Caleb; he and Elena and baby Michael were staying at Caleb and Irina's for the weekend.

The five men took their boots off before tiptoeing up the stairs.

Travis entered the blue room as silently as he could. The bed was empty and the door to the yellow room was closed. Just as he and Sam had agreed it would be.

He set his boots by the bed and went on stocking feet to that shut door. He didn't open it.

But he did stand there for a very long time, wanting to open it, *aching* to open it. And telling himself that wouldn't be right.

Sam woke at six on her wedding day.

She sat straight up in bed and stared at the door to Travis's room.

Shut.

She wanted to leap to her feet and race to that door, to throw it open, and run to him, to climb into bed with him and hold him and whisper…everything.

All her fears. Her doubts. Her scary, nonsensical desire to throw on some clothes, tiptoe down the stairs, sneak out the front door and down the wide steps and take off along the driveway to the road.

To run and keep running.

To never look back.

Until she knew who she was again.

Until she could return to him secure in the knowledge that she was good enough. Ready enough.

Woman enough.

She didn't, though—didn't go to him, didn't run away. She was not only riddled with doubt, but she was also a coward. Which was why she lay back down and closed her eyes and drifted off into a fitful, unhappy sleep until eight, when Mercy came to get her.

Sam put on some jeans and a cotton shirt and followed Luke's wife down the back stairs and out the back door where a limo was waiting, Aleta and Sam's mom, Keisha and the Terrible Twins already inside. The limo rolled along the single-car pebbled driveway that circled the house and then down the wider driveway to the road. Keisha said what a great day it was for a wedding. Aleta and Mercy agreed. Sam's mom was subdued. Dina and Mila were downright civil. They giggled about how cool it was, to be chauffeured in a limo.

Not once did they snicker behind their hands.

Sam realized she was glad they were there.

The limo took them to Gabe and Mary Bravo's ranch, where Travis's sisters and his other sisters-in-law were waiting. And not only all the Bravo women.

There was a surprise guest. He emerged from behind Mary's Christmas tree a moment after Sam walked in the front door. He wore forest-green trousers and a festive red shirt—and the rhinestone suspenders she'd sent him when she mailed him the card inviting him to the wedding.

Sam did not burst into tears at the sight of him. But almost. "Oh, Jonathan. I didn't think you'd come!"

"Darling, I wouldn't have missed this for the world. I called Travis when I got your invitation. He had Mary get in touch. She graciously offered me accommodations here."

Sam hugged him, hard. "Oh, I'm so glad to see you."

"Don't crush me, my love. You simply don't know your own strength." He wiggled from her grasp and smoothed his big hair.

Mary announced that breakfast was served. They all filed into the large, comfortable dining room and sat down to eat.

The food was really good, but Sam was too nervous to eat much. Jonathan, seated on her right, leaned close to her and told her not to pick at her meal. He said she needed food in her stomach.

In spite of the tension that tugged at the muscles between her shoulder blades and tied her belly in knots, she laughed. "I never thought the day would come when you would tell me to eat *more*."

"That is exactly what I'm telling you," he replied. "There is nothing as unattractive as a weak and peckish bride."

She wrinkled her nose at him. "Peckish?"

"Irritable from lack of proper nourishment," he elaborated in the snooty tone of voice she'd come to love.

So she did what he told her to do and ate some more. There was something so comforting about having him there. She could almost relax a little. After all, like Travis, he knew who she really was. He'd been there with her when she made all the changes that had led her to this day when she would become Travis's wife.

Travis's wife. It seemed so huge and impossible. Panic clawed at her again.

She ordered it to be gone.

After the meal, the stylists, cosmeticians and nail techs arrived. Mary played an endless stream of holiday music and everyone got manicures and pedicures. And hair and makeup, too.

Travis's sister, Zoe, was a semiprofessional photographer. She took a lot of pictures that morning. She would photograph the wedding party, too.

Jonathan, in his element, supervised the general beautifying. He advised the twins on nail colors. "Not that one, my sweet. It looks like dried blood—type O, I'm sure. This is your sister's wedding, but she's not marrying the Lord of the Night. Let's go for something a tad less...vampiric, shall we?" He also suggested that Sam's mom wear her hair in soft waves around her face rather than the tighter curls she usually went for. Both the twins and her mom did what he told them to.

There was just something about Jonathan. He knew how to bring out the best in a woman, and women, no matter their age, sensed that. They tended to trust his judgment without question.

A light lunch was provided at noon.

And then it was back in the limo to return to Bravo Ridge.

By one-thirty, a half hour before the simple wedding ceremony, Sam was dressed in her bridal finery and pacing the floor of the yellow room. She was beyond nervous by then, and more panicked than ever, so lost in her own anxiousness that she almost didn't hear the light tap on the door to the hallway.

But then the tap came again.

She called, "Come in."

Her mother, in a pretty lavender mother-of-the-bride dress, slipped through the door. She carried a large rectangular box in one hand and a bag in the other. Both the box and the bag were of shiny cobalt-blue foil, and both were tied with ribbons in white, silver and various shades of purple.

Sam got the picture. It was time for whatever special surprise Aleta and her mom had cooked up between them so that Jennifer would feel she'd contributed to the wedding.

Her mom sighed. "You are a vision."

Sam felt the knot of tension in her stomach loosen a little. Okay, she and her mom had never enjoyed that close of a relationship. And Jennifer could drive her crazy with her constant advice on how to be more feminine, with her passive-aggressive remarks that made Sam want to shout at her to cut the crap and man up.

Still, Jennifer did care. It was so obvious from the hopeful, yearning look on her still-pretty face, from the way her little hands shook just a bit, ruffling the ribbons on the blue foil bag.

Sam gave her a big smile—a real smile. "Thanks, Mom."

Jennifer swiped away a tear with the back of the hand that held the beribboned bag. "Come…let me show you." She turned for the bed and sat on the edge of it, setting the box to the side and holding the bag so carefully in her lap. Sam went and sat down beside her. Her mom handed her the bag.

Sam fiddled with the ribbons. It took forever to get them untied. But her mom didn't try to interfere the way she usually would. She sat there, her hands in her lap, until the ribbons were all undone. Sam sent her a questioning look then. But Jennifer only smiled.

So Sam reached in and took out a blue velvet box. She opened the lid to find a bracelet sparkling with alternating clear and purple gemstones.

"It was *my* mother's," said Jennifer. "Diamonds and amethysts." Amethyst was Sam's birthstone. And she'd been named after her mother's mother. "Your grandmother Samantha's birthstone was amethyst, too—here. Let me put it on you." Solemnly, her mother lifted the bracelet from the box. Speechless, Sam held up her arm and her mother hooked the little heart-shaped platinum clasp at her wrist.

The diamonds sparkled at her, bright as the one in the ring Travis had give her. Sam spoke in a voice that was thick with emotion. "It's so pretty."

"I wanted you to have it. As they say, 'Something old.'"

"Oh, Mom..." Sam reached for her mother.

"Samantha..." Her mother hugged her back.

It was a great moment. One to remember and treasure. Just her and her mom, with all the tough years and the bad feelings put aside. The knots of tension within her seemed to loosen just a little. And the panic, at least right then, had subsided to a vague shiver of unease.

There was more in the bag, something borrowed— her mother's diamond earrings. And a blue garter. Sam donned the earrings, eased the garter up under her dress to mid-thigh.

And then her mom gave her the box.

Sam opened it with the same slow care she'd used to untie the ribbons on the bag. Inside, was a large blue book.

Samantha and Travis...

"Aw, Mom. A scrapbook..."

"It's not finished yet. The last third is empty. That will have the wedding pictures, and the honeymoon, too, and I'll do more work on the cover, once I get the pictures of both of you..."

Sam turned the pages. She touched the lock of her own baby hair, the tiny pink sock and the little yellow bib.

There were lots of pictures of her growing up. Pictures of the Sam she always used to see when she looked in a mirror—the Sam some people mistook for a boy. There were pictures of her in her mom's arms. And with her dad at the ranch. Riding Old Jay, her favorite gelding, and sitting in the back of her dad's pickup in a plaid shirt with the sleeve's torn off. There was even a picture of that awful birthday weekend not all that long ago, and of the cake her mom had made to look like an oil rig, the twins in the background, sticking out their tongues.

Her mother put her arm around her. "You were always such a very capable child. So…self-sufficient."

She leaned into her mother's embrace. "Yeah, I was that."

She moved on to Travis's section of the book, saw his baby pictures, a blue sock, and a bib that was yellow, like hers. His brothers and sisters were in some of the pictures. She turned the pages and watched her love grow into manhood, saw him in his graduation cap and gown, in a tux, holding out an orchid corsage, and in a hard hat and coveralls on the rig at her dad's ranch.

"Aleta sent me everything for Travis's section," said her mom. "She really is one of the kindest, most generous women I've ever met…."

Sam looked in her mother's eyes. "We can all learn a lot from her." She said the words and then tensed, sure her mom would take it wrong.

But her mom only nodded. "Yes, Samantha. Yes, we can."

They sat there, for a few more minutes, just the two of them. Sam started at the beginning of the scrapbook again, looked at every memento, every snapshot, one more time. Then, with loving care, she put it back in the blue box and folded the tissue paper smoothly around it.

"I want to show Travis," she said.

"Of course. You can send it back to me later, along with the pictures and any keepsakes from the wedding and after."

The wedding and after...

After, when she and Travis would be married. Together. Bonded for life before the whole world.

Was that what scared her, what made the panic rise? She knew then, with certainty, that it was not.

Her mom told her again that she was a beautiful bride. "I wish you all the happiness your two hearts can hold," she said. "I wish you more patience than I ever had, more wisdom. And I'm so glad that you and Travis are longtime friends and well-suited. Sadly, your father and I weren't suited at all. But you will do better, I know it in my heart."

So strange and wonderful that her own mom, who'd never in her whole life seemed to understand her, should suddenly be saying just the right things.

Sam said it again, "Thanks, Mom."

And then Jennifer was rising. "I love you," she said. "I wasn't always there when I should have been. And I didn't always love you as you needed loving. I know that. But I did love you. I *do* love you, Samantha. And I always will."

"I love you, too, Mom."

Jennifer went on tiptoe and Sam bent down so that her mom could kiss her cheek. It seemed to Sam a kiss of blessing, a kiss of acknowledgment and acceptance. At last.

Her mother slipped out the way she had come.

Sam stood there, by the bed, unmoving, until there was another tap at the door.

It was Mercy. She looked terrific in midnight blue. "Oh, you look beautiful."

Sam mustered a smile. "Thanks."

"Want some help with your veil?"

Sam went to the vanity set, took the short layers of organza banded with rhinestones and pearls off the edge of the mirror and handed it to Luke's wife. She pulled out the padded stool and sat.

Mercy pinned the veil in place and Sam took the hem and guided it over her forehead, smoothing the ends so it just covered her face. "Perfect," Mercy said.

Sam sat for a moment, gazing at her own reflection in the mirror, thinking about her mom and her dad, about Keisha and Walt. About the Terrible Twins and all the Bravos, every one.

And about Travis, most of all.

Then she pushed back the stool and rose again. She took her bouquet of orchids and white roses from the stand on the tall dresser.

"Ready?" Mercy asked in a hushed, excited tone. At Sam's slow nod, she added, "Your dad's waiting at the top of the stairs." And then she was gone.

Sam's heart started racing and her hands, around the base of the bouquet, felt suddenly clammy. Her feet in her gorgeous rhinestone-accented wedding shoes seemed nailed to the floor.

But somehow, she did it, she lifted one foot and then the other and within ten steps, she was at the door. She pulled it open.

And even with her heart going spooked-rabbit fast, pounding a furious drum roll in her ears, she could still hear the wedding march, floating up from the living room downstairs. And there was her dad in his best black wool suit, standing at the top of the staircase.

He saw her and offered his arm.

Her pulse rat-tat-tatting in her ears, she went to him and hooked her arm in his.

He said, "There's my beautiful, big, strong baby girl."

And she loved him so much right then. He smelled of cigarettes and the moth balls he stored that old rarely worn suit in and she realized he was one of the dearest, truest men in the world.

Almost as dear and true as Travis.

He turned, taking her with him, starting down the stairs.

It was like a dream, only not a dream. A real-life sort of dream. She floated down the stairs on the arm of her father. The carved double doors to the living room stood wide.

They went through, and began the walk up the blue velvet aisle between the rows of white rented folding chairs. Her family and Travis's family rose and turned to watch her progress.

Travis waited at the other end.

In his eyes, she saw so much love.

And worry, too.

For her. For the doubts she saw he knew that she had.

He knew because he knew *her*. He accepted her completely.

As she was now. As she had been. As she would be in the future as the years fled by—so fast. Too fast.

Oh, she could see it all. And it was good. It was right.

She was the Sam she had always been. Strong and tall and able to stand toe-to-toe with any man. She hadn't lost herself after all.

She was exactly who she'd always been.

And yet, because of Travis, because of what they were together, she was also so much more.

It wasn't anything to be afraid of, these changes that

seemed to deny who she was. Because they didn't deny her, not really. They only made her *more*.

She reached his side. The nice minister Aleta had found started to speak.

But Travis put up his hand. The minister fell silent. Sam gave her dad her bouquet to hold for her and her dad stepped away.

Travis took her fingers, guided her to face him. He took her veil and lifted it, smoothing it back over the crown of her head and down. Now nothing stood between them, not even that transparent film of bridal white.

He took her hand again—and then the other hand, too. And his eyes were on her, holding her gaze. He whispered, "Are you sure? Are you absolutely sure? Because I know I pushed you to get married too fast. And if it's just too soon for you, we can call it off right now. It's all right. I'll understand. I can wait, Sam. I see that now. Until you're sure, no matter how long it takes, I'll wait."

An hour before, she might have nodded. She might have told him she couldn't do it, she needed more time.

But something had happened—in those precious moments with her mother, and at the sight of her father. And also, well, just because there is a time in a woman's life when she has to push her deepest fears aside.

She has to say, yes. Absolutely. I will. I love you. I will join my life with yours. And we will make something better and stronger together than either of us could ever be on our own.

This was that time. And Travis was the man. The right man for her.

She told him, "Yes, Travis. I'm sure. I love you. I want to marry you. I want to marry you right now."

He let out a slow breath. "You mean it. You really mean it."

"I mean it." And she kissed him, even though they weren't even married yet, even though the minister hadn't been allowed to say a single word.

No one in the white chairs so much as moved or made a sound—not that Sam cared much what the family did. For her, it was all about Travis. All about the kiss.

When the kiss ended, he said slowly and clearly, "I love you, Sam Jaworski."

"And I love you, Travis Bravo."

They turned together to the waiting, slightly baffled-looking minister. "Go for it," Travis told him.

A wave of laughter rose from the family behind them. More than one of them applauded.

And then the minister began, "Dearly beloved, we are gathered here together..."

Sam said her vows out loud and proud and sure.

Travis's voice was lower, softer, but no less certain. He had the ring ready. He slid it onto her finger, snug against the engagement diamond he'd given her before they knew it would all end up being for real.

And when the minister said, "You may kiss the bride," Travis pulled her close and settled his mouth on hers so tenderly, in a kiss that promised everything—his strong hands and his good heart. All the years of their lives.

And his love, most of all.

It wasn't until they turned back to face the family that she noticed her dad had disappeared. Mercy stood in his place holding out her bouquet.

Sam reached to take it.

And out the arched front windows, the fireworks

began with a bottle rocket shooting toward the wide Texas sky.

Sam growled low in her throat. "He'd better not burn anything down, or I swear I will kill him."

Travis only laughed and pulled her close for another tender kiss.

* * * * *

Watch for the next story
in the Bravo Family Saga.
The Return of Bowie Bravo
is coming in February 2012,
only from Harlequin Special Edition.

HEART & HOME

Heartwarming romances where love can
happen right when you least expect it.

Harlequin®
SPECIAL EDITION®

COMING NEXT MONTH
AVAILABLE NOVEMBER 22, 2011

You can find more information on upcoming Harlequin® titles,
free excerpts and more at www.HarlequinInsideRomance.com.

HSECNM1111

REQUEST YOUR FREE BOOKS!

2 FREE NOVELS PLUS 2 FREE GIFTS!

⬥Harlequin®

SPECIAL EDITION

Life, Love & Family

YES! Please send me 2 FREE Harlequin® Special Edition novels and my 2 FREE gifts (gifts are worth about $10). After receiving them, if I don't wish to receive any more books, I can return the shipping statement marked "cancel." If I don't cancel, I will receive 6 brand-new novels every month and be billed just $4.49 per book in the U.S. or $5.24 per book in Canada. That's a saving of at least 14% off the cover price! It's quite a bargain! Shipping and handling is just 50¢ per book in the U.S. and 75¢ per book in Canada.* I understand that accepting the 2 free books and gifts places me under no obligation to buy anything. I can always return a shipment and cancel at any time. Even if I never buy another book, the two free books and gifts are mine to keep forever.

235/335 HDN FEGF

Name	(PLEASE PRINT)	

Address		Apt. #

City	State/Prov.	Zip/Postal Code

Signature (if under 18, a parent or guardian must sign)

Mail to the **Reader Service:**
IN U.S.A.: P.O. Box 1867, Buffalo, NY 14240-1867
IN CANADA: P.O. Box 609, Fort Erie, Ontario L2A 5X3

Not valid for current subscribers to Harlequin Special Edition books.

Want to try two free books from another line?
Call 1-800-873-8635 or visit www.ReaderService.com.

* Terms and prices subject to change without notice. Prices do not include applicable taxes. Sales tax applicable in N.Y. Canadian residents will be charged applicable taxes. Offer not valid in Quebec. This offer is limited to one order per household. All orders subject to credit approval. Credit or debit balances in a customer's account(s) may be offset by any other outstanding balance owed by or to the customer. Please allow 4 to 6 weeks for delivery. Offer available while quantities last.

Your Privacy—The Reader Service is committed to protecting your privacy. Our Privacy Policy is available online at www.ReaderService.com or upon request from the Reader Service.

We make a portion of our mailing list available to reputable third parties that offer products we believe may interest you. If you prefer that we not exchange your name with third parties, or if you wish to clarify or modify your communication preferences, please visit us at www.ReaderService.com/consumerschoice or write to us at Reader Service Preference Service, P.O. Box 9062, Buffalo, NY 14269. Include your complete name and address.

HSE11B

*Lucy Flemming and Ross Mitchell shared a magical,
sexy Christmas weekend together six years ago.
This Christmas, history may repeat itself when they find
themselves stranded in a major snowstorm...
and alone at last.*

*Read on for a sneak peek from
IT HAPPENED ONE CHRISTMAS
by Leslie Kelly.*

Available December 2011, only from Harlequin® Blaze™.

EYEING THE GRAY, THICK SKY through the expansive wall of
windows, Lucy began to pack up her photography gear.
The Christmas party was winding down, only a dozen or so
people remaining on this floor, which had been transformed
from cubicles and meeting rooms to a holiday funland. She
smiled at those nearest to her, then, seeing the glances at her
silly elf hat, she reached up to tug it off her head.

Before she could do it, however, she heard a voice. A
deep, male voice—smooth and sexy, and so not Santa's.

"I appreciate you filling in on such short notice. I've
heard you do a terrific job."

Lucy didn't turn around, letting her brain process what
she was hearing. Her whole body had stiffened, the hairs on
the back of her neck standing up, her skin tightening into
tiny goose bumps. Because that voice sounded so familiar.
Impossibly familiar.

It can't be.

"It sounds like the kids had a great time."

Unable to stop herself, Lucy began to turn around,
wondering if her ears—and all her other senses—were
deceiving her. After all, six years was a long time, the mind

could play tricks. What were the odds that she'd bump into *him,* here? And today of all days. December 23.

Six years exactly. Was that really possible?

One look—and the accompanying frantic thudding of her heart—and she knew her ears and brain were working just fine. Because it was *him.*

"Oh, my God," he whispered, shocked, frozen, staring as thoroughly as she was. "Lucy?"

She nodded slowly, not taking her eyes off him, wondering why the years had made him even more attractive than ever. It didn't seem fair. Not when she'd spent the past six years thinking he must have started losing that thick, golden-brown hair, or added a spare tire to that trim, muscular form.

No.

The man was gorgeous. Truly, without-a-doubt, mouth-wateringly handsome, every bit as hot as he'd been the first time she'd laid eyes on him. She'd been twenty-two, he one year older.

They'd shared an amazing holiday season.

And had never seen one another again.

Until now.

Find out what happens in
IT HAPPENED ONE CHRISTMAS
by Leslie Kelly.
Available December 2011, only from Harlequin® Blaze™

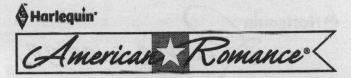

Harlequin

American ★ Romance

LAURA MARIE ALTOM

brings you
another touching tale from

When family tragedy forces Wyatt Buckhorn to pair up
with his longtime secret crush, Natalie Poole, and care
for the Buckhorn clan's seven children, Wyatt worries
he's in over his head. Fearing his shameful secret will
be exposed, Wyatt tries to fight his growing attraction
to Natalie. As Natalie begins to open up to Wyatt,
he starts yearning for a family of his own—a family
with Natalie. But can Wyatt trust his heart enough
to reveal his secret?

A Baby in His Stocking

Available December
wherever books are sold!

www.Harlequin.com

HAR75387

◆ **Harlequin**®

Romance

SUSAN MEIER

*Experience the thrill of falling in love
this holiday season with*

Kisses on Her Christmas List

When Shannon Raleigh saw Rory Wallace staring at her
across her family's department store, she knew he would
be trouble...for her heart. Guarded, but unable to fight
her attraction, Shannon is drawn to Rory and his inquisitive
daughter. Now with only seven days to convince this
straitlaced businessman that what they feel for each other
is real, Shannon hopes for a Christmas miracle.

**Will the magic of Christmas be enough
to melt his heart?**

Available December 6, 2011.

www.Harlequin.com

HRI7769